HOLLOW

OWEN EGERTON

SOFT SKULL PRESS
NEW YORK

Library of Congress Cataloging-in-Publication Data Is Available.

Cover design by Matt Dorfman
Interior design by Sabrina Plomitallo-González

ISBN 978-1-61902-940-8

Soft Skull Press
1140 Broadway
New York, NY 10001
www.softskull.com

Printed in the United States of America
Distributed by Publishers Group West

10 9 8 7 6 5 4 3 2 1

For Gwyn

My son, are you willing to go with me and explore—to go far beyond where man has ever ventured?   —Olaf Jansen

Abort the day of my birth,
        black out the night I was conceived.
May God say, it never was.
                —Job

THE MOMENT YOU WERE BORN, THE ROOM SMELLED OF WARM SOIL and blood.

The moment you were born, I was so surprised I hiccupped. A dozen what-to-expect books, nine months of pregnancy, seven hours of labor, and I was surprised.

The moment you were born, I understood you would fill my spot on earth, and in the same way you had popped into existence, I would someday pop out.

The moment you were born, a crying laugh rumbled in my chest and I knew I would do anything for you.

But I didn't.

That was three years ago.

NORTHWARD

MY NAME IS OLIVER BONDS AND I BELIEVE THE EARTH TO BE HOLLOW.

I understand this is not a widely held belief. Three years ago the idea would have inspired only my contempt but it has become a fundamental conviction of mine.

I live alone in a shed behind Jenny's Beauty Salon in south Austin. It's a single room with a cot, a mini fridge, a camper stove, and a sink that no longer works. Currently the shed is padlocked from the outside.

This happened late yesterday afternoon. I had just filled a pot of water from the shower when someone knocked on the shed door.

"Bonds? Bonds, are you in there?" It was Mr. Miller, my landlord. He's the one who added the plumbing and mini-fridge. He charges $100 a month. It's not much, I know, but I haven't paid in two months. "Bonds, I've got a padlock. I'm locking her up, so if you're in there, you best come out."

I like Mr. Miller. He has a laurel of grey hair and an Irish accent barely bruised by twenty years in Texas. I would have opened the door, but I had nothing to give him and nothing to tell him. I stood frozen with a pot of water, not daring to breathe.

"I'm serious, Bonds!"

I once lived three blocks from here in a two-story brick house with two oaks in the backyard and a custom built porch. Carrie and I moved in the same year we were married. We decorated and refurbished, on our knees late into the night varnishing the hardwood floors, making our way through a bottle of red wine, and singing along to David Bowie playing on an iPhone. We lived there for years. It's where we conceived. It's the house we brought our baby Miles home to. It's where our baby died and it's where we fell apart.

Miller was quiet now, listening for me. I was stuck. Open the door and face my guilt or become a prisoner. The question has obvious existential implications, but knowing that didn't help.

A minute ticked by as Miller listened for me. I stood watching the water in the pot, concentrating on keeping its surface still. Miller could have opened the door and walked right in, it wasn't locked. But Miller has an old world courtesy and a begrudging respect of other people's privacy. The decision to act or not was mine. But I didn't make a decision. I just didn't move and eventually I heard the click of a padlock and Mr. Miller's receding steps.

Only after he'd been gone several minutes was I able to place the pot down. I boiled the water and prepared some ramen noodles. I showered and went to bed early.

Hours later I woke up to the sound of steps just outside my door. Then four loud knocks. I lay in my cot, not daring to move. Whoever it was said nothing, only rattled the padlock and grunted. What kept me in was keeping him out, and that was fine by me. Whoever it was stood there for a few minutes before banging on the door once more. Then he left and I lay awake until the dark greyed into morning.

Small morning birds yip in the pine tree just behind the shed. It's a tuneless noise. There's a high window in the shed, a little larger than a laptop. I shove the cot under the window, push it open, and lift myself through. My feet leave the cot and my torso dangles outside. I balance, unsure what to do next, then fall.

It's a soft enough fall, but I don't rush to stand. I lie on the damp, sandy soil and watch the eggshell sky through the pines. It's only just morning, that lukewarm hour when the sky comes to be but the sun has yet to rise. Mr. Miller has locked my shed and I have less than twenty dollars to my name. This was inevitable. I haven't worked in years. I live a life unsustainable.

When Miles was born, I was sure my income would be too small to cover mortgage, insurance, car payments, college savings, dinners, diapers, vacations, hardback books. I pictured my monthly paycheck stretched over our expenses like a queen sheet on a king-sized bed. I worried and hatched schemes to bring in more cash, real estate and investments that I never quite put into action. I thought we were poor—not impoverished, but poor. But for three years I've lived on the remnant of that income.

I was never able to think about what I will do when the money is gone. I don't mean I couldn't bear the thought, I mean I was, am, unable to imagine a month from now. A week. My mind blurs, like looking into lake water at night.

I get to my feet, brush off the sand, and walk around to the front. Sure enough, there's the padlock. It's the kind used on a middle school locker. The cheapness of it makes me feel worse.

There's also a folded piece of torn paper stuck to the door. From Mr. Miller, I suspect. An eviction notice or a threat or a note explaining how disappointed he is in me. Then I remember my late night knocker. I pull the note from the door. It's been stuck there with a wad of chewed gum. I unfold the paper and recognize the aggressively enthusiastic handwriting. It's not a threat. It's an invitation:

> Oliver—I've got a way to get us into the
> HOLLOW EARTH! All will be revealed!
>
> Lyle

Lyle, of course.

The note may seem extraordinary—a path into the center of the world, adventure beyond imagination, the greatest of mysteries uncovered. But any excitement is tempered by the fact that Lyle is a liar. He's also my best friend.

I first met Lyle in a used bookshop a little over two years ago.

After Miles died I stopped reading. I purchased books, opened them, turned their pages. I still fell asleep with an open book on my chest nearly every night. But I never read a word past the title, and often not even that. Reading lets it in.

By then, I wasn't living with Carrie. I had moved into a chain motel off the interstate. At the time, I called it a dump. Today it would be a resort.

I no longer went to the university. For a time I had, but it was a charade. Me sitting at my desk doing nothing. Not teaching, not talking. Students walking in and finding me unresponsive. The university never actually fired me. They remained largely silent during the investigation. A university waits for history to decide itself before it speaks. We preach nothing, happily affecting nothing.

Instead of the campus, I spent my days in a used bookstore built in the shell of an old supermarket. The high ceilings still lined with the bright white supermarket fluorescents. Shelves of books nearly touching the ceiling formed paths and nooks. Standing before a wall of books, my half-distant look was completely appropriate. I was just another browser.

I'd pick out a book—something thick with a hardback binding, and I'd sit, staring into the pages and they'd all leave me alone.

On a warm day in mid-April, I had been at the bookstore for an hour with a mildewing book from the vintage section. I gazed past the typed words, letting them all blur, letting my mind be nowhere—the Buddhists would have celebrated my mindlessness.

"Breast milk is a lie."

I looked up to see this large man looming over me. He was six foot and just on the safe side of three hundred pounds, his baggy jeans rolled an inch above his ankles as if ready for wading through shallow waters.

"Excuse me?" I asked.

"Breast milk," he said, pointing at my book, which turned out to be a scientific treatise on the benefits of breastfeeding. "Never drink it. Didn't drink it from my mom and I sure as hell don't drink it from a cow."

"Oh."

"If you knew a faucet would run dry after nine months or so, would you install it? Would you teach your children to drink from it? Rely on it?"

"It lasts longer than nine months. I mean, people breastfeed for much longer, years sometimes."

Miles was still breastfeeding before he died.

"That's why America is so backward. Bunch of citizens addicted to their mom's teat and wondering why they can't pass Algebra. A.D.D, my ass. We're distracted by our own buried childhoods. Were you breastfed?"

I nodded.

"See?"

I did not nod.

"Look at me! A head taller than you, easy. No breast milk. That stuff stunts you. In the 50's, we knew it. We were perfecting formula. Then hippies started shoving their boobs in babies' mouths again, and look. Vietnam, Iraq, Afghanistan."

"I'm not following you."

"That's it! Perfectly it! You're looking to FOLLOW! Because, fuck, you were your mom's bitch from day one. I'm solo. Stand on my own. I do not follow! Even if I like the direction, I won't follow. But we've got a nation of followers."

"I wasn't really reading it."

"Ha!"

"I don't read anymore. I just pretend to." I had never said this to anyone. But this man, even if he did judge, what could it mean to me? This has remained the power of our friendship. He is full of opinions and I don't value his opinions.

"Why don't you read?" he asked.

"My son died."

"Oh," he said with a nod, as if this made sense. "Maybe you just need a better book. Follow me. Come on."

My therapist, when I could afford her, told me it was healthy for people to respond with concern or sympathy. But I hated it. So when this guy only nodded and led me to the Esoteric Science section of the store, I followed.

"*Hollow Earth: Theory to Fact* by Dr. Jim Horner," he said, shoving the book in my hand and placing my breastfeeding book in the empty spot. "It's going to blow your fucking mind."

I took the book and thanked him.

He stuck out a large hand. "Lyle," he said.

"Oliver," I said. "Oliver Bonds."

"I avoid last names." He knocked his knuckles against the book. "Get ready. Everything you think you know is wrong."

I walk north from the shed toward the river and downtown. New sunrays, just higher than horizontal, filter through the trees, and droplets of rainwater still clinging to oak leaves hold morsels of the light. Morning birds yip. By day's end they'll be grackles, coughing calls and rising from the trees as one, a black floating shadow. But for now, they're just morning birds.

I pause at the Sunflower Daycare, a small, high-priced, downtown daycare, and I watch the blonde boy playing in the sandbox. He must be almost three. His head is curls and his laugh is a gurgle. I watch him each morning through the bars separating the sidewalk from the playscape. The young women overseeing the play glance my way uneasily, but I stay. The blond boy pushes a yellow truck through the sand and blubbers the engine. He builds a mountain, a dam, a city of sand. The blond boy destroys it. He builds it again.

This is my wife's son. He doesn't know who I am.

Among the downtown buildings, people are already making their way into Starbucks and through revolving doors and up escalators to higher floors. I've learned that the higher floors are reserved for those who have money. I am no longer asked past the 2nd floor of any building. In fact, I'm heading to a basement. St. Christopher's Episcopalian Church donates its basement to a homeless resource center—the Agape Center. They usually have food. If nothing else, they'll have coffee.

I walk past the church's off-white steeple, small in the midst of the mirror and metal of the surrounding city. Due to the slant of the hill the church is built on, the basement has street access on the south side. A solid dozen people are already lining up, leaning with their bundles of blankets and coats against the outside wall. I take my place at the end, nodding morning greetings. By 8:30, the line will wind around the building.

If you're in line before 7:30, you can usually get a breakfast. They only allow sixty people in for breakfast. It's all the cold boiled eggs and bagels they can afford. I know this because Carrie and I used to volunteer one morning a week. It was part of our adult Bible study.

Murray waddles up behind me. Murray has spent years perfecting a traditional homeless look—sprawling gray-black beard covering his face nearly all the way to his dark, darting eyes, the yellow-brown skin glossy with grime, and the acidic smell of cheap alcohol filtered through abused sweat glands. He sports a long black trench coat that he endures even in the summer's heat and a felt hat that looks like it was picked off the corpse of a Confederate general.

He mumbles, his words a high-pitched whine muffled by drink and matted facial hair.

"Morning, Murray," I say.

"Why you out here? You're supposed to be in there?" We have this conversation often.

"I'm out here."

"Who's making the breakfast?"

"The volunteers."

"You a volunteer."

"Nope. Just a neighbor."

He laughs.

Behind him comes Ben. Ben isn't old. Maybe forty. He has three teeth and bulging, almost comical eyes. I sometimes wonder that he's able to blink with eyeballs that large. He's carrying a sleeping bag which is unraveling in his lanky arms. He shakes his head as he gathers the bag into his arms.

"How goes it, Ben?"

"Tired," he says. "Had to move from my camp. Some new guy came and stayed up all night yelling. I tried to talk some sense into him, but he kept on. I don't want no trouble, so I got my stuff and left."

"Where are you going to go?"

Ben shakes his head, those outrageous eyes threatening to pop right out of his skull. "No jobs. I don't want to mess up again. I did that, you know. Jail. Thought maybe I had a job at the McDonalds, but I didn't."

Of course he didn't. Ben with his three teeth, ping-pong eyes, and IQ hovering just above the temperature of a rain puddle. What could he do? These days there'll be fifty people, at least, going for that one job. All needing it. Why would anyone hire Ben? They won't. So what's Ben going to do? How is he going to make it? He won't. He'll live in the woods and parks of Austin, Texas, and die out there too.

He shakes his head, gathering his ever-unraveling bag.

"You don't want a job," Murray mumbles.

"I do too," says Ben.

"No you don't. You just want some crack."

"I don't do crack, asshole."

"Yep. Crack and whatever you can get."

Ben looks at me, his eyes pleading. "I'm clean. Been clean a while now."

"That's just cause you can't get anything."

Ben chuckles. "Well, that's kind of true."

At 8:30 the doors open and we shuffle past Chip, the stout security guard who remembers each person's name and greets them with a strong smile.

"Oliver," he says, patting my back. "Good morning."

Chip didn't know me before. That's good. The other volunteers, the ones I used to show up with at 7:45 to slice oranges and squeeze single eggs from a plastic bag of twenty, they can't look at me for long. I feel sorry for them, because they feel sorry for me. Maybe they're a little afraid they'll catch a bad case of homelessness themselves.

But I'm not quite homeless. I have my shed behind the beauty salon with a padlocked door and an open back window. I just come to Agape for the company and coffee.

It's a slow line. We sign in and are handed a meal ticket. We move to plastic folding chairs at plastic folding tables set in two long rows. I add my name to a list requesting a bus pass. It requires a ten-minute meeting with a caseworker, usually Linda. I don't mind. Linda fills me with positive aphorisms and photocopied lists of job resources, then hands me a bus pass and ushers me out. I'm not her most urgent case. I'm surviving.

"Hey," Murray pokes me. "If you're not one of them, who's gonna give the sermon?"

"God will provide," I say. Murray frowns, at least I think he frowns. It's hard to tell with the beard.

When I was a volunteer I often led the morning devotions. Simple messages. A Mary Oliver poem or a story of the chicken-soup-for-the-soul variety. Nothing that would change a life, just some nice words to accompany the coffee. I think, perhaps, I enjoyed giving the devotions more than the neighbors enjoyed receiving them.

I enjoyed most everything about the Agape Center in those days. The quiet of the long, clean kitchen before opening, the deep chuckles of Larry who directed the breakfast preparations, and the rush as 8:30 hit and the line rolled in from the cold, or heat, or rain, and on came the hectic hurry of handing out breakfasts and brewing vat after vat of coffee—carrying a new hot vat out just as the last one spurted empty. I enjoyed the thank yous, the privilege of serving—honestly, the privilege of serving. And at morning's end, I went home and took a nap.

We sit and wait in the plastic chairs for the announcements and devotion. It's crowded today, people eager for a dry spot after last night's storm. The rain has brought out the stench. I smell better than most, thanks to the shed's shower. And my clothes are not smeared with street, that smell of stale rainwater and beer.

Some here are old, broken people whose minds no longer work if they ever did. Some are so gut-sick on alcohol their mouths don't work, others are clean and well kept—homeless in disguise. There's the Austrian woman who had a nervous breakdown in Salzburg. She left her family and found herself in America without a work visa. "I had never even slept outside before. Never been camping." Passing her on the street, you'd never guess she lives in the woods by the railroad tracks. There's Pete who bartended in Austin's Bourbon Den for thirty years. When the bar closed, he was in his mid-fifties and couldn't find another bartending job. Mac served in Iraq, Liz was pregnant at thirteen, Dale still wears the suit from the job he lost two weeks ago. They don't all have reasons they are homeless any more than one has a reason they work for this company or that.

I sit beside Hector, a one-armed Hispanic man buried in an oversized black coat. He smells awful this morning. Not just the street or the rain or the stink of days camping on end. Not even feces or urine. It's something I don't recognize.

"Morning Hector," I say. He looks at me with small, dark eyes and an angry brow. Hector doesn't speak much.

Charlie, a plump and over-eager, middle-aged seminary student, stumbles through a mini-sermon and Miriam, the cropped-haired center director, announces there'll be free reading glasses given out today. I can't think for the smell.

"And now, let's break bread together," Miriam says and we rise and shuffle through another line, handing in our meal tickets for a breakfast served in a red and white paper tray—a boiled egg, a bagel (a tortilla for those whose teeth, or lack thereof, can't handle a bagel), three cubes of bright orange cheese, a dollop of peanut butter, and a slice of fruit. Some days we get day-old pastries donated from Starbucks or Whole Foods.

I keep my head down, my eyes low. The woman behind me, her mouth a toothless gap, frowns at her tray. "Apples? Apples? I can't eat apples. I need yogurt."

I fill a mug of coffee and return to my seat. Hector is already eating, bits of coffee-wet bagel sticking to the thin hairs of his mustache. A tin of cheap tobacco and papers lay before him. The man rolls his own with one arm, spending much of his time at Agape on the front steps rolling and smoking. I wish they'd let him smoke inside. The burn would cover the smell.

I stare at my food. I stare at the egg. Hector's smell is green and encompassing.

He places his own boiled egg into his mouth in one bite, then maneuvers out of his jacket as he chews. With the jacket off, the stench doubles. Then I see his arm.

A rag covers the elbow stump of his left arm. Rubber bands strap it tight around the nub. The rag is damp, a wet yellow-red stain squeezed off by the rubber bands. Hector is rotting.

No one else sees, he's rotting as he picks at cheese cubes and a bagel. He's rotting before he's dead. He's rotting like Job. I try and breathe and I cannot. I can see the maggots. I know I can't, but I do.

"Hector," I say. He turns to me, his face twisting in disgust. "Hector, your arm."

Hector reaches onto my tray, taking my egg and shoving it into his already full mouth.

"They're eating your arm, Hector."

His eyes flick so angry I find them confusing. He opens his mouth and spits chewed egg over my face. I cough backward, standing and tipping my chair.

Hector returns to his breakfast, but Chip is there in seconds, a heavy hand on Hector's shoulder, pulling him to his feet and escorting him toward the door.

"Hector, you can't be doing that," he says. "I have to ban you for a week, okay? You can't come back for one week, understand?"

I take my seat. I fail to remove the egg and spit on my face. Instead I watch pieces of egg float in my coffee like tiny icebergs. People chatter about me, grackles void of melody, loud and pointless and terrifying. And I feel a horrible tickle.

It's my only warning. A wave is coming.

Miles's not-being seeps through me like veinless blood. It is the color of everything, the taste of everything. But at least once a day, often more, Miles's death strikes present and new. Not mourning, not the throb of grief. This is scalding panic. The water retreats giving me just enough warning to do nothing, and then the wave hits, drowning everything.

People snicker, cough, a phone rings, a coffee cup spills, I grip the table and hold my breath.

Like a sledgehammer moving through my chest. Any healing is crushed, the scar tissue ripped away, and the wound gapes fresh.

I remember his smell.

I'm still gripping the table when they call my name to see the case-worker.

I STEP INSIDE LINDA'S OFFICE. IT'S A SMALL ROOM SMELLING OF WOOL and Lysol. Linda isn't here yet, so I sit before her desk and listen to the tiny coffee maker burble in the corner.

"Sorry I'm late," a voice says behind me. "Not used to this traffic." It's not Linda.

She rounds the desk, her eyes on a stack of paper in her hands, and I see her before she sees me. She looks older, but still very young. Her hair, black and long, gathers in a tail that slinks over her shoulder.

Ashley.

She sits down behind her desk, still not fully seeing me. "Now, let's see what we can do for you." She looks up and stops. Her eyes a dark hazel, like polished wood.

"Dr. Bonds?" she says cautiously. Her face has grown sharper, her gaze more stern.

"Where's Linda?" I ask.

"Took a job in Dallas, I think. I just started yesterday." Her voice is the same, light with the slightest scratch.

I nod. I nod for longer than I should. "Bolivia?" I manage.

"Yeah," she says with a slight smile. "For a bit. Then grad school after all. Social Work, University of Oklahoma."

I nod, but that's it. I can't seem to talk. Not to her.

"It's good to be back. Tulsa is no Austin."

Her smile tilts, closed and knowing, sliding up her cheek and into the dimple of her heart-shaped face. Perplexing. I find her perplexing.

"One of the clients here told me it's better to be homeless in Austin than rich in Tulsa." She laughs. I can't even do that. My silence is brittle.

"Didn't expect to run into you," she says. "But I guess coincidence is God's way of remaining anonymous." She shrugs. "You said that once in class."

"Einstein said it." It snaps out of me.

"I never had him," she says. "Would you like some coffee?" She stands, moving to the small coffee maker. She'd bring coffee to my office. Two cups from a local shop on the Drag.

"Black with a pinch of sugar, right? Got to have the sweet to appreciate the bitter. You said that, too."

"My father used to say it. I stole it from him."

She hands me a napkin. "You have a little something on your face."

She stands before me as I wipe the egg away and crumple the napkin into my pocket. She holds out the mug. I take it in both hands and stare down into the black. She moves back to her chair. This is her office. Her office hours.

"So . . . how are you?" The question strikes us both as ridiculous and we smile. Me first, her following.

"I need a bus pass."

"Dr. Bonds," she says, quietly.

"You can call me Oliver."

"Are you all right?"

I look up. She's sterner, yes. Last time I saw her, her naked body was ogled by a room of unsmiling people.

"Just a bus pass," I say, looking back into my coffee. "That's all I need."

She opens a draw and pulls out a blue and white Metro bus pass. She pauses, looking at it, then hands it over.

"Are you researching a book or something?"

I take the pass. "A lot has happened," I say.

"Okay," she says, as if I'm beginning the conversation. But I stand to leave.

"I work here now," she says as I open the door. "I'm here every day."

I close the door behind me.

"Mother was a suicide." That was Ashley's wording on her first visit to my office.

No 'my' before 'mother.' 'Suicide' used to denote the person, not the act, as if she were a Faulknerian heroine and not just a senior religious studies major.

"I'm sorry," I say. This happened. Students coming by office hours to discuss a grade or upcoming assignment then slipping into confessions and life stories. I didn't mind. I could play secular priest.

"She believed in the bible," Ashley said.

"Many people do."

"I don't." She sat up straight, as if only now she was ready to address the business at hand even though we'd been talking for fifteen minutes. "Today in class you said the Book of Job wasn't true."

"I said it was a fiction, not that it wasn't true." I sat straight, too, pleased to be back in the subject I taught. "It wasn't intended to be a history like Chronicles or Exodus or even the gospels. It's a poem built around a question."

"Why do people suffer. Got that," she said. "And it's because God and Satan make a gentleman's wager, right?"

"That's the folktale," I said with a chuckle. It was arrogant chuckle. A I'm-about-to-lay-down-some-teaching chuckle. "The folktale of Job is much older than the poem. It acts as the framework for the debate. Imagine taking a story everyone knows, Cinderella for example, and sandwiching in the middle of the story a long, philosophical discussion between Cinderella and her stepsisters on the nature of happiness and privilege. The author of Job did the same thing. Took a well-known story about a good man made to suffer, but who maintains his faith in God. He's eventually restored and God gives everything back."

"That's the part I hate."

"Which part?"

"The ending." When she frowned one thin line stretched across her young forehead like a fault line, narrow and unalarming, but promising some distant future quake. "God kills Job's kids, or lets Satan kill them, then says, 'Hey, here's some new kids. No harm done.' It's like some drunk dad buying his kid a candy bar after slapping him around."

"You could read it like that," I say, smiling.

"And Job is fine with it."

"That seems to be the implication."

"So?" she asked.

"So?"

"So what's the answer? Why do people suffer?"

"Well, the book is more extraordinary for the question than the answer."

She frowned again.

"Job was written to a people who understood that God rewards the good and punishes the evil. We suffer because we've done something wrong."

"We've *sinned*." She said it with a near-sneer.

"But Job knows he has not sinned. He's a faultless man. And it terrifies him."

"He's terrified because he's innocent?"

"Because he's being made to suffer for no reason. He begs God to show him his sin. '*Make me to know my transgression and my sin!*' If he's guilty, at least the universe still makes sense. But he knows he's innocent. So God isn't rewarding the good and punishing the evil, after all. Suffering is much more random. For Job this is more horrifying than boils and grief. Everything he thought he knew about how the universe operates is smashed."

"And his friends?"

"Job is being punished, that's clear to them. Therefore he must be guilty. They spend pages urging him to come clean and confess."

"And his wife?"

"She's more practical," I said. "She gets one great line in the whole book. Then basically disappears. While everyone else is clearing their throats preparing for thirty-nine chapters of theological debate, she sums it all up with one piece of advice. '*Curse God and die.*'"

Ashley nodded, that same one-line forehead frown. "That's the advice my mom took."

SEVERAL THINGS ARE HAPPENING.

Bentley gives a talk about the major entrances into the hollow earth—he stands narrow and nervous.

Next to me, Lyle whispers insults and observations. "Jesus, this guy's a dicknut."

From down the court a voice yells, "Take the shot!"

The Hollow Earth Society of Central Texas usually meets in a reserved classroom at the downtown Austin YMCA. But a glitch double-booked the room so instead we sit in six metal folding chairs centered in the south end free throw lane of YMCA's basketball court. This would be fine if it weren't for the three-on-three pick up game on the north end of the court.

"Just ignore them, everyone," Belinda, our heavy and motherly president, says. She closes her eyes and breathes. Then she smiles at Bentley and nods for him to continue.

"Now, as I was saying, there's more than one way inside, we know that. The question I pose to you is how many ways?" As Bentley speaks his eyes dart and his jaw clenches between the words. His shyness is stringent as onions, but he insists on giving a lecture at least once a month. He plucks out certainty like it's a tune he's learning but will never master. I admire him.

"Take the shot, Brad! Take it!"

"But after researching—"

"Go! Go! Go! Shoot!"

"—researching several webpages and a scientific journal, I've come to the disturbing conclusion—"

A basketball from the north end slams into Bentley's head.

"Ball help," a twenty-something in a headband calls. His friends chuckle. Bentley trots after the ball.

From beside me, Lyle sighs loudly and crosses his arms across his bulk. "Don't get it for them, Bentley." But Bentley continues.

The twenty-something opens his arms and Bentley hurls the ball. The ball travels five feet before bouncing awkwardly and rolling past the twenty-something who stares at Bentley with contempt.

"Keep going, Bentley," Belinda says. "You're doing fine."

"I'd like to propose that many of the smaller entrances to the hollow earth are closing. Some naturally and some by order of the world government. It's common knowledge that Egypt's walled up the entrance in the subterranean levels of the Giza pyramid. I propose soon the only available entrance will be the Symmes Holes. And those must be kept safe. But I don't see how anyone —even the covert world government —could clog a hole a hundred miles wide?"

"It would kill the planet," Gilly says. She's thin with a tight face and wide eyes.

"It *would* kill the planet! Like clogging an artery," Bentley says. He picks up a pile of photocopied pages. "I've made a list of the dwindling suspected entry points across—"

Smack. The basketball hits his shoulder and sends the papers flying.

"Ball help."

Again, Bentley trots after the ball.

"Bentley," Lyle says. "They're doing it on purpose."

"Kindness breeds kindness," Bentley says quietly as he rolls the ball to the twenty-something.

"Maybe you could meet somewhere else, dude," says the twenty-something, who I assume is Brad. "Less danger of getting hit."

"Sir," Belinda twists, her chair squeaking under her. "We have as much right to be here as you do. We have reserved this spot."

The twenty-something grunts and turns back to his game. Belinda smiles and nods at Bentley. Moments like this are exactly why we voted her president.

"So the question is whether our window into the hollow earth is shrinking." Bentley picks up the papers carpeting the court. "Could it be that we only have decades left to contact our brothers below?"

"I've had psychic contact twice." Gilly says.

"I'm referring to physical contact."

"That's small thinking," Glenn, Gilly's equally thin husband, says. "That was a fucking foul, Brad! Watch the elbow!"

"I don't mean to dismiss psychic contact. It's just—"

"Well, you kind of did dismiss it," Gilly says. "You kind of called it stupid."

"I didn't say it was stupid."

"You implied it."

"You did kind of imply it," Glenn says. "You kind of made that face."

"What face?"

"That face a person makes when something is stupid."

"I'm sorry if I made that face, Gilly. Really."

After first meeting Lyle in the used bookstore, I didn't see him for several days. But I did take the book he handed me - *Hollow Earth: Theory to Fact* by Dr. Jim Horner. That same night, in the low light of my damp motel room, I opened the book.

"There is no greater threat to the continued evolution of human-kind than unquestioned beliefs," Horner begins. "The most insidious of these beliefs is that our planet is a solid ball and we its sole sentient residents. If you believe that, then nearly everything you think you know is wrong."

I read these words and my heart tingled. If there was one thing I had learned it was that everything I knew was wrong.

Horner goes on to trace the history of hollow earth theory from Tibetan beliefs in the inner paradisal city Shambhala to the ancient Greeks myth of the underworld, on to notable scientists championing a hollow earth model like astronomer Edmund Halley and mathematician Leonard Euler, and American free-thinkers like Captain John Cleves Symmes, Jr. who theorized in 1818 that the clearest path into the hollow earth were massive holes located at the north and south pole.

The argument is simple. Our earth—in fact all planets—are by nature hollow. Hollow and inhabitable with an eco-system separate but symbiotic to our own.

Due to its mass and the centrifugal force of the earth's spin, the majority of gravity is found not in the core, but in the earth's crust. So we walk on one side of the crust, and those within walk on the other side of the crust. Though it appears some creatures—devolved humanoids—dwell in cities carved into the crust, the majority of non-surface life thrives on the concave inner-surface.

All of this, of course, flies in the face of most modern geologic models, which is why scientists have such a difficult time accepting it. As Dr. Horner puts it, "It is a bold mind that willingly forsakes the false science of their fathers."

My father taught me that hard work is justly rewarded and there's no such thing as a free lunch. I've seen much work go unrewarded and I have eaten many free lunches.

Modern explorers have searched for a way in, either through the Symmes Holes at the Poles or in deep caverns, ancient temples, or even ocean canyons. We have a few testimonies of lost ships and submarines disappearing to parts unknown, but nothing conclusive enough to dismiss the skeptics.

What lies within? What kind of life exists in the rays of that inner sun? Some say that our inner world is a primitive place, like surface life in the last ice age with prehistoric animals hunted by tribes of peaceful humanoids. A few fear an advanced race with demonic intentions. But most experts believe the inner earth to be the home of technologically and spiritually advanced beings that have evolved past war, past poverty, past mortality.

Our government—from NASA to the military—openly ridicules hollow earth theory. In his book, Dr. Horner explains that in fact the government is well aware of the hollow earth and the wide pole entrances. They have long suppressed satellite images of the poles and narratives of sailors and scientists who have stumbled into that hidden world. The government believes the stark truth would cause massive panic on the surface. "Once we know we are not alone in this globe, economies will crack, religions will crumble, and the status quo will cease to be. No wonder those in power are so reluctant to have the truth revealed. When you discover that the unimagined is fact, the first reaction is panic."

I know this to be true. After Miles died, my own footsteps made me flinch with fear.

Dr. Horner concludes his book with a promise to acquire a nuclear-powered icebreaker and lead an exploration into the northern Symmes Hole himself so that the hollow earth can move from theory into known fact.

"We are ripe for a revolution of thought, no less radical than the Copernican revolution."

I read all of Horner's book in one sitting, the words dripping into my head like water into a kettle that has burned itself dry. I, too, was ripe for revolution. I was blank and newly uncertain of the nature of everything.

Lyle found me at the bookstore days later. I was sitting in a corner rereading Horner's book. He hovered above me until I looked up. He nodded knowingly and said, with an exaggerated drawl, "See?"

For weeks after we'd sit over waffles or bubble tea and he'd talk ceaselessly about the hollow earth, spouting off half-facts and theories and conspiracies, and lending me dog-eared books and smudged DVDs. *A Guide to Inner Earth* by Bruce A. Walton; *A Journey to the Earth's Interior: Or, Have the Poles Really Been Discovered* by Marshall Blutcher Gardner; *Flying Saucers from the Earth's Interior* by Raymond W. Bernard; *The Kingdom of Agarttha: A Journey into the Hollow Earth* by Marquis Alexandre Saint-Yves d'Alveydre.

As if a fire had swept away my mental library, these books repopulated my mind's shelves. I understood it was all pseudo-science, but I liked it. I liked listening. I was like a child appeased by a new book read aloud.

I once taught in my Introduction to World Religions class that no person is ever truly without some kind of faith. The sternest of atheists and the most dedicated of rationalists all have faith.

Even outside of organized religion, we gravitate to religious practices: an exercise routine, a morning newspaper, a weekly therapist appointment. We form congregations with likeminded thinkers. And we believe that these practices and these opinions somehow give our life meaning. We are, I taught, religious by nature.

And when one's understanding of how the world works shatters, we lose our opinions and practices, and we are excommunicated, either voluntarily or by force.

A void is formed. Something will fill it.

If Lyle had been Jehovah's Witness or a Hare Krishna, would I be sitting in a different YMCA room?

I doubt it.

Hollow earth struck me in a way no official religion could. For starters, I know too much about religion. I'm an expert with a PhD to prove it. You can't tell anyone anything about what they believe they already know. And secondly, at the center of the hollow earth conversation is a question, not an answer. The belief held by all hollow earthers is that the globe is hollow. The real question is what resides within. I can embrace any faith that revolves around a question.

The concept of the hollow earth was something better than factual; it was applicable. I was myself a hollow shell with nothing but a question at my core.

"Okay," says Belinda, placing her palms together. "We're almost out of time. It's a game night and the Little Dunkers get here at six. But before we close up . . ." Belinda pauses and smiles at me. "As you know, Jim Horner's North Pole exhibition is on schedule for this coming spring. As we also all know, Lyle has applied— "

"Hell yes, I have," Lyle says through a grin.

"But Lyle wasn't alone from our group." Belinda turns to me. "Oliver, I hope it's okay I let the cat out of the bag."

"What cat?" I ask.

"Seems Oliver has also applied. Both he and Lyle have been selected to join Jim Horner - two of only two hundred accepted applicants."

I look to Lyle, who grins. This explains the note on my door.

"Are you going?" Bentley asks me.

"Are we going?" Lyle says before I can answer. "Bentley, you back ass, of course we're going."

"It's ten thousand dollars a person."

"Oooo," Lyle says. "I'm terrified." He stands, dwarfing Bentley. He opens his arms to take in the group. "A chance to shake hands with a higher race and come back with pictures and proof and tell all the fuckers you were right? I think ten K is a bargain. Ollie thinks so too, don't you?"

All those eyes on me. I open my mouth, but I see the basketball flying towards the back of Lyle's head. "Lyle," I say.

He turns just in time and catches the ball with one large palm.

"Ball help," Brad says.

Lyle places the ball down on his seat and reaches into his backpack. "I tell you. I'm not sure if I want to come back, maybe we'll get there and just take up residence."

"Dude. Ball help!"

Lyle pulls a switchblade from his bag.

"Dude."

"Now, Lyle," says Belinda.

Lyle raises the switchblade. "Because I'm getting pretty fucking tired of this side of the crust." He slams down the blade into the basketball. It hisses and drops limp to the floor. The twenty-something steps away.

Lyle smiles at all of us. "We'll send you a postcard."

"Lyle, what did you do?" I ask as we step out of the YMCA. The day is muggy, a heat building beneath a smear of gray sky.

"I got you a fucking seat to the hollow earth." He lights a cigarette. Lyle will usually squeeze in two in the fifty feet between the door and his car. "I think I deserve a thank you."

"I never applied."

"I saved you the trouble." He hikes up his blue jeans. "We should hit IHOP. They're starting that pumpkin pancake special."

"Lyle, I don't have any money."

"We'll split an order."

"That's not what I mean."

We climb into his blue Geo Metro, Lyle curving his body over the wheel in order to fit. The floor is carpeted with empty cigarette packs, butts, and ash. It's like having your feet in the remains of Pompeii. But I don't drive anymore, so I can't complain.

"You used to have money, huh?" Lyle asks, pulling out of the parking lot. "Did the court take it away? Or was it your ex?" He lights a new cigarette, steering with his knee.

"It just didn't last." I say. "Lyle, I can't go on an expedition."

"This is Dr. Horner we're talking about, Ollie. Dr. Jim Horner chose you!" He beats on the wheel like it's a bongo. "The main focus for us is raising that money. Ten K times two. We can sell blood, sperm, etc. Maybe pick up some side work. We've got to think big."

"Lyle, I'm not going."

"Before I forget, at IHOP you're sixty-five."

"I'm not even forty."

"There's a senior citizen deal and you look older than me. I'll be your son. No, too predictable. I'll be your nephew. Or maybe I'm dating your daughter."

"I don't have a daughter."

"It's our backstory. You've got to have a backstory."

"Welcome to the International House of Pancakes," our waiter wheezes. "Do you know what you'd like?"

He's round. His face is scarred with acne. It's like watching a fleshy moon. I imagine him as a teenager, maybe ten years ago, in the stink of a public high school bathroom glaring at a mirror, his face revolting against him with bumps and sores. I see him very alone.

"Hello," Lyle says with a large smile. "We'd each like to order a pumpkin special. And we'd like the senior citizen discount. Does that come with coffee?" Lyle looks to me. "Uncle Peppy, can you drink coffee?"

"Wait," says the waiter, one eyebrow struggling to rise. "He's a senior citizen? Really?"

"Yes." Lyle can lie with perfect eye contact. It's his greatest talent.

The waiter grins, making the red constellations on his face rearrange. "I don't think I can swing that for you guys."

"My uncle fought in Korea and you're going to charge him full price for pancakes?"

The waiter sighs and turns to me. "Do you have any ID?"

I reach into my wallet, but I keep my eyes on his red face. How can a person grow when so many looked away? What chance did he have? He should have had a chance.

"I'm sorry about your face," I say as I give him an ID card.

He frowns at me. He has a dimple.

He looks at the card. "Okay, student discount. Two specials for the price of one." He walks away without waiting for a reply.

"Ollie, what did you show him?"

"University Staff ID. It's all I've got with my picture on it."

"Sweet!" Lyle says. "We are eating pancakes every day this week."

"Okay," I say. "Explain the application."

Lyle puckers his lips in thought and fixes his gaze on me. The waiter places down two coffees and a plastic carafe, and Lyle's still staring. Then—like a snap—he simultaneously begins talking and pouring sugar into his cup.

"Confession time," he says. "I applied for me, right? Only for me. But 'pedicab operator' doesn't look that impressive on the application. So I borrowed some of your credentials. Not a lot of legit PhDs bold enough to join the hollow earth faction. Too dependent on mommy *univer-titty* to go against the mainstream fantasy. But I didn't use your name. Not at first."

"Yes?"

"They checked the references!" Lyle lifts his arms as if this was a faux pas of grand proportions. "Can you believe that? I'm trusting these guys with my life and money, and they don't even believe my application."

"To be fair, you were lying."

"They didn't know that." He reaches across the table and snags a handful of individual creamers. "You think a machine fills these things? Or is it someone's job?" He pops the first creamer straight into his mouth.

"So you came clean?"

"I told them I had been filling out the application for you and accidentally put my name down." He alternates, a creamer for the coffee, a creamer straight shot. "So they gave us two spots. Dr. Oliver Bonds and his guide-man."

"I have a guide-man?"

"You're blind." Pop into the mouth. Some drips land on his chin. "Since birth."

"You want me to pretend to be blind?"

"Only for the first week." He gulps half his coffee in one swallow. "Then I figure we stage a miracle cure. Maybe we say it was the aurora borealis or something."

"Once I'm a seeing man, won't they kick you off the boat?"

"By then I'll have proven my worth. I mean, I know my shit, right? I just don't have some fancy paper from some ass-knocker establishment. No offense."

The waiter arrives with two plates of yellow-brown pancakes sprinkled with tiny candy pumpkins. I look from the pancake to the waiter's face. They could be brothers. He walks away.

"I'm not going," I say.

Lyle crisscrosses syrup over his cakes. "It's a journey into the hollow earth, Oliver. You have to go."

"I don't have any money. I'm no longer a working professor. My application was entered under false pretenses. And I doubt the validity of the entire venture."

Lyle speaks through a mouthful of pancake. "That's your uncle speaking."

"I don't have an uncle."

"I'm quoting *Star Wars*."

"Don't."

Lyle frowns. "Give me one good reason not to go."

"I just gave you four."

"Fluff." Fork in hand, he waves the waiter over to refill his coffee.

"Lyle," I say. "I have responsibilities."

His wave to the waiter spins into a point directed at my face. "No, Oliver, you don't. That's the point. You don't have anything." He forks half a pancake and lifts it. It wiggles like a disembodied flipper pulled from a gulf oil slick. "Convicts settled Australia. Madmen crossed the Atlantic. Ne'er-do-wells went west for gold. People with nothing to lose." He shoves the flipper into his mouth. "Guys like you and me, we're made for this kind of shit."

I raise a bite, stare at it, then place it back on the plate.

He's right, I know. No one is asking me to stay. No one relies on my contributions. I could go anywhere and no one would blink.

"Look," Lyle says. "Your kid died. I get that. Hell, if I were you, I would have—" Lyle shapes his hand into a gun and puts it to his temples. He pops his lips as he sends a mime bullet soaring through his skull. "But," he says. "You're still among the living, Ollie. So you might as well do something. You going eat that?"

He reaches over the table and spears the top pancake.

"I tell you what. Read this." Lyle retrieves a hardback book from his backpack and slaps it on the table between us. The cover reads *Our Journey In* by Dr. Jim Horner. "It's an advance copy. He mailed a copy to everyone going on the expedition."

"I didn't get one."

Lyle shrugs. "You're blind." He swallows a mouthful. "He's coming to Austin on the book tour, too," he says. "We'll get to meet him."

I pick up the book. It shows a globe with a hole emitting streams of light. Even now I feel that quiet thrill any unread book holds.

"Ollie," Lyle says, pushing in the last of the pancakes. "If you're looking for answers, there's no better place to look than the center of the world."

WITH HORNER'S NEW BOOK IN ONE HAND, I WALK THROUGH MY neighborhood. I move past the houses and pollen-coated lawns, breathing in the damp heat and ozone. The late-day sun dips away and everything turns amber—the trees, the air, the cracked sidewalk. Everything hums. The old woman, who lost her husband four years ago, waving at the children climbing from an overused trampoline; the near-blind fifty-year-old decked in denim and a greying beard who tromps from the convenience store with a six pack of tall boys and a red-tipped cigarette; the new couple from California pushing a stroller the price of a secondhand SUV. The dentist waters his lawn avoiding the cacti, and the banjo player strums on his deck as cats leap from the banister. I live among these people. Some still know my name.

A few clouds roll over the last of the sunlight and everything dims.

Here's the house that was once my home. Where we lived, Carrie and I and Miles.

It looks good. The new owners have undone most of our renovations. Repainted the door and replaced the lawn with xeriscaping and a rock garden. I see him occasionally—a dark-haired man with high eyebrows. I've only seen his wife in shadow, passing by windows and turning off lights.

I wonder if I'm there too, a ghost taking shape. In my head I'm there so often. I'm there right now.

There was the immediate urge to die, the morning I found him. Then later in jail.

Days passed, I did not die.

I did not die for Carrie.

Later, for a brief time, I did not die out of spite.

Before long, the pain changed. It throbbed more than stabbed. And the dramatic act of taking my own life slipped out of reach. It wasn't that I wished to live so much as I was not willing to die. Not then, at least.

A moan comes from the yard next door to my former house. A cry to a yell to a deep and long almost animal growl. The sound doesn't end, it tumbles forward into nonsense syllables like a baby's babbling but with a grown man's tone. It's Jeffrey.

The yard's fence is tall, tight. Narrow yellow lines of light and the unmelodic song passes through the slits between the planks. I stop and listen.

Jeffrey must be nearly nineteen now. He must be big. By age fifteen he was over two hundred pounds and taller than me. On occasion, years back, I would sit on my back porch, sipping a beer, pretending to enjoy the dusk light, but staring at the wooden planks of the fence that separated my yard from theirs. He paced, unseen, behind that seven-foot fence, wordlessly calling. I don't know if he was crying or talking or trying to name clouds.

Once I came home from work and found Jeffrey standing in our living room—looming and rocking on the heels of his shoes.

"Jeffrey. Hi. Are you visiting Carrie?" He held a porcelain elephant figurine, the size of a toaster. A heavy, cumbersome thing usually residing on the couch's end table.

"Carrie?" I called. Jeffrey stared at the elephant as if he were going to try and solve it like a Rubik's Cube. "Carrie, you home?"

I took a step towards the bedroom. Jeffrey barked at me—a seal's bark more than a dog's. I froze.

"Everything is okay, Jeffrey." I put my hands up and stepped back. "Now, do you know where my wife is? Where Carrie is?"

Another bark. Louder. Hoarse.

We stood in that room unmoving. The air conditioning clicked on. I tried to think.

Then the front door opened behind me. Carrie came in with a bag of take out.

"Hi," she said, looking from me to Jeffrey. "Hi, Jeffrey. Here for a visit?"

"Wait," I turned to her. "You didn't let him in?"

"I just got here."

"Jeffrey," I said as calmly as I could. "How did you get in here?" Groan.

"I'll go get his dad," Carrie said, and I was alone with him again. He bounced the elephant in his hands as if he were guessing its weight.

"It was a wedding gift," I said, stupidly.

Within a minute his father rushed in with Carrie behind him. He shook his head at me apologetically, a big man with a football player's build and few smiles for anyone.

"Come on Jeffrey, let's go," he said. "That's not our elephant. Come on."

"He can keep the elephant," I said.

"Come on Jeffrey, Come on. Give back the elephant."

Jeffrey lifted the elephant above his head. I waved my wife back.

"Jeffrey. Give that elephant back!" his father said.

"Really," I said. "He can have it."

His father grabbed the figurine and yanked. Jeffrey bellowed.

"Let it go," his father said through clenched teeth. "Now. Let it go."

Jeffrey did and his father stumbled back with the elephant, almost falling. He handed it to me and I felt oddly guilty.

The father turned back and took Jeffrey's wrist, leading him to the front door. Jeffrey tried to brace himself at the door and his father pulled. Then Jeffrey went limp like a non-violent protestor and sat on the floor.

"Can I help?" I asked, cradling the elephant. The father ignored me. He wrapped his body around his son in a kind of professional wrestling move and maneuvered him through the door. Not violent, not out of control. His father was meticulous, careful, but not gentle. It occurred to me he had done this before, that perhaps he had taken classes on how to remove his son physically from situations, that perhaps this was a daily routine. In jerks and yanks, Jeffrey's father moved him out the door, Jeffrey barking and grinding his teeth.

"Bye," I said as Jeffrey and his father limped out of our yard like some four-legged, two-headed mythical beast. It seemed equally rude to shut the door or watch the struggle.

Carrie stood beside me. She looked pale.

"There but for the grace of God," she said quietly and closed the door.

Now on the sidewalk, all these years later, I listen to Jeffrey's bellowing. It hovers high, for a moment, wavering like the final note of an opera. It's a song of sorts. I never heard it like that before. Jeffrey may be crying, but he is singing too. He's singing louder than I ever dared.

I stand and listen and the song continues as the first drops fall on the cement and the back of my hands. Soon I hear the sliding door and Jeffrey's father calling his son in from the rain.

He loves his son. I can hear that in the way he calls. I could see that in the way he restrained him.

We became pregnant in our fourth year of marriage.

We read all the books, studied the medical websites, knew what foods to avoid, what vitamins to take, what yogurts to abstain from. Carrie informed the law firm she would be taking a prolonged leave. My students made name suggestions—Pendragon, Hamlet, Fellini. People gifted us car seats and stuffed Muppets. Even before Carrie was showing, our home began transforming with knick-knacks and diaper pails.

We took a six-week class with four other couples to prepare for birth. Our teacher was a wide-smiling hippie whose home smelled of scented candles and faint traces of pot. We sat in her living room on one of three low, cushioned couches sipping non-caffeinated teas and watching videos of babies being born in hospitals, homes, hot tubs, meadows. We studied the anatomy of the womb with a plastic model. We practiced pain moderating, clutching ice cubes and imagining the colors of pain, picturing the edge of pain, exploring where pain ends.

One evening our teacher gathered the mothers-to-be on the floor in the center of the room. The fathers-to-be (and one "other-mother," as she called herself) encircled them. The teacher instructed us to howl. To howl like coyotes. She gave us an example, tilting her head, straightening her throat, and releasing a long harrowing bawl.

"This is bullshit," whispered the other-mother beside me.

A couple of women jumped right in and began howling. One woman howled with more enthusiasm than any coyote I've ever heard. Others offered quiet moans. Carrie gazed around awkwardly.

"Now the partners," said the teacher, grinning. "You are the protective circle. Howl!"

I watched Carrie, ready to follow her lead. She was on her knees, her hands cradling her extended belly. She smiled at me, almost a snicker, a shared understanding. Then she closed her eyes, lifting her chin to the ceiling and sang out a slow, mournful howl.

For a moment, I only watched. She was so beautiful. So changing. Her auburn hair long against her back.

"Come on, partners," the teacher said. "It's a family song."

I closed my eyes and howled, quietly at first, then louder. The room echoed with howling, a full off-key harmony, strange and good.

Like the storm wind now howling under the loose door of this shed, through the paneled floor, howling with the rain and the first of the thunder.

Carrie howled in labor. She squeezed my fist and grunted, sounds so guttural, so nearly sexual at times I found myself aroused. The hospital room smelled of earth and body, then the scent of soil and blood. She groaned, red hair sticking to her sweat-wet forehead, her eyes rolling back, contractions shaking her like thunder.

For an hour of the labor, she and I stood in the shower of the labor room. She rested her arms on my shoulders and we swayed, like teenagers slow dancing. The water warm over my hands on her back. Her breathing long, slow whistles. Me, nodding agreement in the dark.

Later the contractions grew so intense that I lost track of Carrie. I was beside her, bending close, letting her bruise my knuckles with her grip. But she was somewhere alone. On each push, she dove down deep, far from me and that room, she was inside and finding our baby and carrying him to the surface.

"Now, don't you go holding your breath," a nurse said to me. "I get dads passing out left and right. You just keep breathing."

"Well, I see his head," said the doctor, a balding man with bored eyes. "One little cut and he'll slide right out. You ready for that?" He looked to me and then to Carrie.

"No," Carrie said. "No. I don't want that."

"It'll be over lickety split," the doctor said.

"No," I said.

"Okie dokie," he said.

And she pushed again. And again, calling out.

Carrie hoisting herself up on her elbows and staring down her body, pushing. One last, long push and out you came.

And your mother and I gasping as if a baby was the last thing we expected to see. A red tuft of wet hair on your scalp and eyes squeezed against the light. I guffawed tears.

We knew you immediately. Even then, pink and slick with blood and birth, I knew you. I recognized you, Miles. You cried and wriggled and the nurse placed your small body on Carrie's chest.

Everything was new. Everything.

The rain is falling in earnest by the time I get back to the shed. It falls on the roof like tapping fingers. I pick up Dr. Horner's new book, *Our Journey In.* There's the wonderful soft crack as the new book opens. I sit on my cot and read.

Horner describes the nuclear icebreaker, a Russian vessel called the Yamal. He imagines boarding her and setting our course for the northern Symmes Hole. The rain picks up as I picture the journey.

Northward, toward the Pole.

Ice, a wall of it circling the arctic seas.

Beyond the ice where the sea grows calm and warm.

A whirlpool at the top of the world where the ocean flows into the globe.

Then the inner world warmed by a small red sun.

Horner expects enormous cities of singing giants with technology a millennium beyond our own. He describes how he and his fellow explorers will make diplomatic contact and receive the wisdom of these towering ancients.

"Secrets," he promises.

> All the hidden secrets will be discovered. For this
> is where we came from. The Hollow Earth is Eden.

We on the surface are descendants of all who were cast out. Our journey in is a journey home.

They know we are coming.

In my research I've uncovered interviews with Tibetan Lamas and testimonies that now leave me convinced that in the heart of the Hollow Earth is a massive mirror or screen on which our enlightened inner earth cousins monitor our progress. The Lamas describe this device as a "magic mirror" and promise that it can reveal the future, show the past, or unveil the most unfathomable of mysteries. Is it a colossal computer or a peephole into the workings of reality or is it simply looking into the mind of God?

Imagine staring into this "mirror" and whispering your questions. We will conclusively know the truth about the Kennedy assassination, the Roswell cover-up, and the submerged U.S. military bases. And, of course, we may ask spiritual questions, too. The questions that have plagued humankind throughout history. This mirror holds the answers to our deepest whys.

I close the book. It's raining harder, palms slapping more than finger tapping, water dripping down the wall. This place, this life, it is unsustainable.

Manuel had used that very word. Unsustainable. He told me I had a choice.

Manuel Cruz had been a friend. He led our adult bible study at St. Christopher's Episcopalian Church. A little older than me with a round face and metal-rimmed glasses. Kind eyes, willing smile. I'm not sure if he liked me in the class. I doubt it's fun having a history of religion professor in your Sunday school. I never corrected him or argued. Though perhaps I allowed a smug expression or two to cross my face.

Manuel was, in a very real way, there for Carrie and me in the aftermath. Organizing cooked meals dropped off by church members, phone calls and visits, always available with an open ear and assuring eyes. And when I left and hid away in a cheap hotel room that smelled of mold and heat, he came and found me. He sat on the edge of the bed. I sat in the one chair. It rolled on wheels, a squeak muted by the thin carpet.

"I know it's been hard since Miles passed," he said, looking to my draped window.

I told him I detested the word 'passed.' It implies passing on to something. It tries to pretty up death. Whatever death is, it is not, as the Dalai Lama likes to say, simply a change of clothing.

He asked how I was getting along, had I talked to Carrie, was I getting any help? My answers didn't give him much to go on. I told him I didn't want help.

"You know how you're living, here in this place, you know it's unsustainable?"

I rolled my chair a little to the side.

"I want you to know, Oliver. You're not alone. We're there for you. God is there for you."

"That doesn't make any sense."

"He holds our pain," Manuel said. "He suffers with us."

"I don't believe that."

"Oliver," he said, talking off his glasses. "When my wife died, I felt lost."

I remembered his wife. A serious woman with a small face. She had died in a car accident years before.

"I hated God. Hated that He'd made me a widower, that He'd left my daughter without a mother. Honestly, I was ready to give up."

"You wanted to die."

He squeezed his knees. "I was going to drive into the barrier of the I-35 upper deck split. Built up speed a few times. Got up to over a hundred miles-per-hour and knew I could do it. Just a turn of the wheel."

I watched him for a minute. Then spoke. "I thought about stepping in front of a train."

He nodded.

"But it seemed unfair . . ." I said. "To the engineer."

"Sure."

He put his glasses back on. "I saw I had a choice," he said. "I could give up. I could believe Jenny's death was random and meaningless, or I could believe God had a plan."

"You believe God killed your wife?"

"I believe God orchestrates our lives. There's so much we don't see. So much we won't understand until we're in heaven."

"You believe God killed your wife," I say.

"I believe life has meaning," he said.

"You're telling me to believe God killed my son."

"I'm telling you to choose meaning," he said. "I looked down both paths, Oliver. The one you're on just leads to madness."

If the rain keeps up, the water dripping down the walls will pool across the floor. Everything here is used up. Even the camping stove is running low on propane. Everything is worn out, except this book in my hand. *Our Journey In* is new. There's still a slight resistance in the binding. It's filled with dry, unstained pages promising a path to a mirror and answers.

Manuel told me I could go mad or go God. But there's another option. I'll carry my complaints to center of the world and ask why the world is the way the world is.

In April of 1829, Norwegian fisherman Olaf Jansen and his father's small fishing sloop were blown off course by a tremendous storm. A north wind drove them beyond their maps through green-ice seas of lifeless islands and icebergs the size of London.

They came to a wall of ice stretching across the ocean like the coast of a white-blue continent. As the current drove them hurtling forward, the father spotted a narrow crack in the wall and the two managed to steer into the passage.

The translucent walls strained the yellow from the sun and left the day blue and ethereal. Their boat cut through ice water thick as sludge and into a cathedral of ice with walls reaching higher than the clouds. Their only light was the flat, gray strip of sky above them and the blue-green sunglow of the ice walls. At night the constellations were truncated and strange. The walls, Olaf says, contained hunks of diamonds and garnet and the frozen open-eyed corpses of animals unknown. The ice blurred the bodies so that as the sloop passed the animals seemed to move, to gesture.

After several days the walls grew closer. The current pushed the small boat into a narrowing alley. They argued direction, Olaf wanting to row back against the current, his father urging them on even as the passage shrank. Night fell and the two still fought. Their raised voices echoed back to them, moving through the circles and paths and returning to them foreign as if there were a hundred men, a thousand, lost in these passages.

But at first light came hope. In the near distance they saw an opening in the frozen labyrinth. Before them lay a calm and iceless sea. They breathed in and the air was warm. Pulling water from the sea to wash their faces, they found the water fresh, saltless. And still their compass read North.

HERE'S WHAT THEY EXPECT TO FIND AT THE NORTH POLE

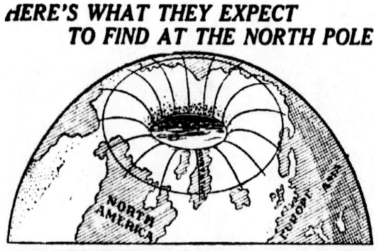

HOW THEY EXPECT TO GET INTO THE HOLLOW EARTH

ICE

In front of us, girding the horizon from left to right, was a vaporish fog or mist. Whether it covered a treacherous iceberg, or some other hidden obstacle against which our little sloop would dash and send us to a watery grave, or was merely the phenomenon of an Arctic fog, there was no way to determine. —Olaf Jansen

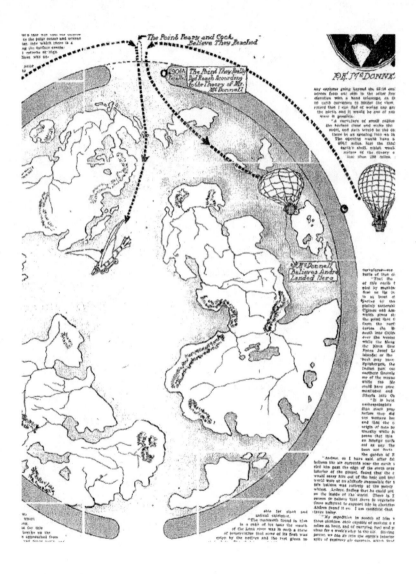

MARTIN AND I WERE KICKED OUT OF AUSTIN HOSPICE THE SAME week. I as a volunteer, he as a low-income patient. Both of us were a little embarrassed.

He lives, for now, up north of 183. It takes two busses and an hour's travel to reach his neighborhood. This is not the Austin you see on postcards. This is second-rate grocery stores, fast food boxes, same day loan banks, and rented squalor.

Martin was my fifth assignment as a hospice volunteer.

Shortly before Miles was born, I went through the two weekends of volunteer training on end-of-life etiquette and was placed on a hospice team. A team consists of a doctor, a nurse, a chaplain, a counselor, and a volunteer. The volunteer's job was the most vague and most varied. I sat with an old yellowing woman in a nursing home as she complained about her sister ten years dead. I gave a shy man with a bloated belly and hardly any words rides to and from his doctor appointments. I took a mentally retarded man who didn't understand he was dying for milkshakes and malt balls for the last three weeks of his life.

For a time I was on the Eleventh Hour Team, awake well past midnight in a hospital room or in an overly warm bedroom beside a mother or father or sister or brother while the family caught a few hours of sleep or a much needed meal. Just my being there gave the families the chance to step out without fearing their loved-one would die alone.

They warned us in our training that often a person chooses these hours to die, the brief spell when family has left the room, as if the pressure is off and they can get on with it.

I walk from the bus stop into Martin's neighborhood. The subdivision had been built forty or so years ago as a suburb for the growing city, quick new houses perfect for the middle class nuclear family. But poverty and time beat the shit out of the neighborhood and broke its face. Paint peels, roofs sag, windows break and are repaired with strips of duct tape. Broken couches, appliance parts, and uncollected trash tumble from the curb onto the street and the air is ripe with garbage and anger and fear and need. They watch me as I walk, wondering what I might take from them, or what they might take from me.

When the newspaper ran the stories of Miles's death and my arrest, hospice stopped calling. Much later, I called them once and asked why. The volunteer manager, a bright-voiced Buddhist woman, told me she thought it best if I take a break from hospice.

"But I'd like to volunteer. I'm willing."

"Quite honestly, Mr. Bonds, we have to question your competence. We have the safety of our clients to consider."

"It's hospice. What's the worst that could happen?"

Martin was still my patient at the time. He had been for over a year, long past the six months his oncologist had given him to live. That's why he was kicked out.

Hospice is pretty strict about who gets care. If a doctor gives you more than a year to live, you're a no-go. Hospice is for the dying.

At first Martin was dying just fine. Cancer—born in the lungs but expanding all over with its own manifest destiny. His doctor gave him six months to live and recommended hospice care. Six months came and went. As did a year. Martin was still alive. The doctor shrugged and was later convicted for possession of cocaine.

Martin got a new doctor who prescribed a complete chemo program. To qualify for hospice care, you can't be seeking treatment. You have to be a lost cause. They're not trying to be cruel. They have to have standards or everyone with a sniffle would sign up for care.

So within four days of the other, Martin and I found our association with Hospice Austin severed. We decided to keep our friendship going outside of hospice jurisdiction. He didn't mind that I had been accused of homicide and I didn't mind that he had failed to die on schedule.

Martin lives in one side of a duplex made from what used to be a family home. The cracked driveway holds a late model beige Cadillac with two flat, rotting tires and a raised hood. Three or four guys from the neighborhood are staring in. These men are strong and often high. It's Martin's car, but it hasn't run in a year.

"Holy shit! Ollie!" Martin says after swinging the door open. He always acts surprised. But I'm here the same time every week. He hugs me. He's wet, nothing but a towel wrapped around his waist, yet he still smells of smoke.

Martin's thinner. He's always thinner. I can see the plug where they inject the chemo. It protrudes from his chest like an old-fashioned car cigarette lighter. It grows more prominent as he grows less so.

He's a small man to start with, maybe five foot five. He swears he was taller before the cancer. I don't see how that's possible.

"Come on in!" he says. "Hey, Sam. Ollie's here."

A tall man sits shirtless on one of the three leather couches crammed into the living room. Sam is built like a high school athlete ten years past two-a-days. Thick arms, fist-sized pecs, with a pooch just above his silver skull belt buckle. His shoulders are wide and inked with cheap tattoos—blurred like a sharpie sketch on a paper towel. The depiction of some rodent—a rat or opossum—screeches on his chest, its ribbed tail stretching up and around his neck.

He nods at me. His eyes don't trust me, never have.

Sitting in a ball on the couch, her eyes on the screaming television, is a woman I don't know. She's thin, pale skin like a threadbare sheet that's lost its color in the wash. She's wearing a nightshirt pulled over her knees.

The front door closes and the room is darker. Heavy curtains cover the windows. Besides the television, a single bulb in the open kitchen is the only light. The space is thick with smoke that has no room to float. It hangs static in the air.

"I'll get dressed. Hold on here. You want a beer?"

I don't drink. Martin knows this, but he offers to be polite.

"Okay, okay. I'll be right back. I am starving," he says as he heads down the hall to his room in the rear of the house.

Sam sometimes rents a room from Martin. He sometimes disappears. He spent a month in jail last year for hitting a girlfriend.

"Lying bitch," he had said. "Hit herself with a bat and said it was my fist. Judge didn't even ask. Look at my right hand. I can't even make a fist. The bones never healed right."

The woman's face changes with the light of the television. It's a divorce court reality show—a couple yelling, a judge frowning. She watches intently, her mouth slightly ajar.

"Met a college kid doing stand up," Sam says, not looking up from the pink pills he's lining on the coffee table. "Asked him if he knew you. He didn't. But I don't know your last name."

"Bonds."

"He didn't know you," he says. "Funny guy."

"Oh."

"I'm doing some stand up now. Kind of a career change."

The woman turns her head and looks at him, the television flickering against her face like malformed ghosts.

"Don't you worry," he says without looking at her. "I'm not retiring yet."

Sam smirks at me as if we're sharing a joke. I look to her, but she's returned her gaze to the fighting couple, now scratching at each other.

"You teach history?" Sam asks, opening a new bottle of pills and beginning a new line.

"Religion," I say. "History of religion. I used to."

"Shit. I'm a history buff." He smiles. "You know the Civil War?"

"I'm aware of it."

"Aware of it. Shit." He shakes his head. "I've read a dozen books on it. A dozen easy. Read two biographies of Lee. One on Lincoln. You know what was the craziest? The prisons. I found this book in the prison library all about the POW camps. You know, for the captured soldiers. I swear we've never treated foreigners as bad as we treated our own. Both sides, too. Concentration camp stuff. Starved corpses stacked like wood, you know. No food, no room. All the water clean as piss."

I'm watching her. In her twenties, I guess. As the images on the screen grow more frantic, she grins. One tooth is coffee, the others are small and off-white.

"How the fuck did that book end up in a Texas prison library? You think they wanted us to feel better about Del Valle?" Sam chuckles, recounting the pills with his fingers. "Over fifty thousand died just in the prisons. One place, Camp Sumter, killed off nearly every soldier who went there. Starved them, froze them, let them rot in the mud. When it was all over, the guy who ran it got charged with war crimes. He was the only person in the whole Civil War who got charged for war crimes. They hanged him."

"I didn't know that."

The show has gone to commercial and the pale woman turns to listen to Sam. I try not to look at her. I concentrate on Sam's tattoos, that ribbed tail snaking up his neck.

"The guy was a doctor. From Switzerland or something. I love that. The worst villain of the Civil War was some Swiss doctor. Had a gift for torture. Didn't know he had it, then the opportunity came and he knew just what to do to make it hurt bad." He nods to himself.

I turn my head and see that the woman is staring at me. I look away, then back. She's still staring, unsmiling and unmoving in the agitated light of the television. I stare back. Her eyes are cloud gray.

Sam finishes counting and jumps a little in his seat. I break my stare and shove my hands in my pocket. Sam flicks his chin back to Martin's room. "How's he doing? Better."

"Worse, I think."

"He's gonna beat this. I know that."

A used tissue lies on the carpet at my feet. I step on it.

"All right," Martin walks in wearing ironed denim jeans and his old motorcycle jacket. He used to fill it, I imagine. "Let's go."

"How much you thinking, Martin?" Sam asks.

"Ah, shit. Same as last time." Martin looks to me, embarrassed. He sells his meds, I know. We never talk about it.

I glance back at the woman. She's flipping through channels, her head bent as if she's trying to decipher the images.

Martin and I walk the three blocks to Burger King. We take our time.

"Oh, man, Ollie. I am ready for this. A big meal. Yes, sir."

"Who's the woman?" I ask.

"Who? Laika? Really interesting girl. She's from Russia."

"Is she a spy?"

Martin laughs until he coughs. "She's a good working girl," he explains with a wink. "Sam does a little organizing on the side. He's like her agent, if you get my meaning. She's super interesting."

I pay for his burger. A habit left over from wealthier days.

"It's good to get out," he tells me. "Just good to be out in the world."

Watching Martin eat is hard. He wants food, but his body doesn't. He keeps trying to trick himself into eating. He takes half an hour building up the burger, adding ketchup, salt, pepper, a few well-placed dabs of mustard, Thousand Island dressing until the bread limps soggy. The whole time he's smacking his lips, "This is going to be good. Oh, I've been needing this."

I pace myself, eating slowly, careful to make the fries last. But I'm still nearly finished by the time he's ready to take his first bite.

When he finally lifts the burger, the bread is falling away in sad, damp clumps. He shoves the burger into his mouth, but his body immediately fights him. Even as he chews, his tongue works against him pushing the food out. He smiles. He swallows. He gags. More than once he's thrown up on the tray. He doesn't today and I'm grateful.

"How was chemo?"

"Missed it. My ride never came."

"Again?"

"I know. I know." He puts the burger down. "Hate that chemo. Hate it. Makes me sick. Makes me worse. When I was just dying I got better. Now I'm trying to get better and it's killing me."

"Still smoking?"

"Yeah, yeah. But I roll my own now, so that's a step."

"Isn't that worse?"

"No way. It's the filters that give you cancer. That and all the chemicals. Menthol, that'll kill you quick."

He picks up the burger, letting it hover heavy and wet. He takes a nibble, then places it back down.

"I think I can get that Caddy rolling. I really do. Sam knows his engines. Used to work on cars. He promised to lend a hand." He nods down at the burger and picks it up again. "Yeah, get it running and take a road trip west. I got a buddy in California always saying I should stay with him for a while. Take the Caddy out west then up the coast on Route One." He smacks his lips. "That's the plan."

I know that car will never run. Martin may know this too. But like that burger in his hands, he has a knack for believing the best of a situation.

He puts the burger down, picks up a fry, and takes a bite. "Man, that is good." He puts the other half of the fry back on the tray.

BACK AT HIS HOME, MARTIN PLACES A BURGER KING BAG OF UNEATEN food in his fridge and I follow him to his room in the back of the duplex.

Martin keeps his room immaculate. A tightly tucked NASCAR blanket covers his double bed. A worn out leather recliner, too big for the room. Several *Motor Car* magazines are perfectly stacked on a table beside a frequently-emptied ashtray. A collection of miniature die-cast automobiles preserved in their boxes are carefully arranged on a shelf. Beside them are three framed photos: a nephew, an infant niece with her parents and Martin's mother, and one of him as a younger man on a motorcycle. In this last photo he's healthy and nearly unrecognizable.

He sits in his recliner and coughs.

"I've got some news, Martin. I've been invited to join an expedition into the North Pole."

"Is this that middle earth shit?"

"Hollow earth." I clutch the golf club, a driver that leans against the corner.

"There's a door up there or something, right?" he asks.

"A hole," I say, gently swinging the club. "Big enough to sail into."

"It's butt cold up at the North Pole, you know that, right?" He leans back, popping up the recliner's footrest. "You should go west with me."

I sit on the edge of his bed and tap the club against the carpet. "Martin," I say. "If you could ask God any question, any at all, what would it be?"

Martin thinks for a long beat, then sniffs. "Nothing."

"Nothing?"

"I figure He's got a plan. I don't need to know it. It'll all work out," he says.

"That's not true. Not even a little."

"Sure it is."

"You think there's going to be some third act twist that makes all the horrible things in this world seem okay?" I say. "That's a lie."

Martin stares silently. Then grins. "Hell, Ollie. No wonder you got fired from hospice. You're depressing as shit."

I stay until Martin falls asleep in his leather chair, his breath raspy and strained. I slip through his bedroom door, quietly closing it behind me.

"He's sick?"

The Russian prostitute is waiting in the hall by the door to Sam's room. She stares at me with the gray eyes and I wonder how long she's been waiting.

"No more than usual," I say.

"He'll get better. He's strong."

Did she learn that kind of lie in the States, or is it universal to pretend we don't die?

"You're Oliver, yes?"

Why am I nervous? Sex, I guess. The twitch in my belly in the ninth grade while talking to a girl who it was rumored had given three football players a blowjob. Someone unrestrained in the face of my restraint. They always seemed somehow magical, enchanted. This gray enchanted thing.

"Yes. Martin told me," she nods, her brown tooth flashing as she speaks. "I'm Laika."

We're still in the hall, her body close, though she is in no way trying to seduce me. Her shirt is loose. I can smell her, sour sweat and tobacco.

"How do you like America?" I say because I have nothing to say. "Do you like the food?"

"Yes," she says with all sincerity. "I do like the hamburger. And the taco. Not the pizza. But yes, the hamburger." She nods for a moment and lights a cigarette.

"Do you have family back in Russia?"

"No," she says. "Why did you ask me that?"

I pause. "I don't know."

She frowns.

"I should get going."

I move past her, that same sour smell simultaneously revolting and arousing me. She follows.

"I don't always do this."

"Do what?"

"Fuck. Fuck for the money," she says. Speaking it out loud is strange. Like a one-legged man referring to his limp.

"There's no shame in it."

"If there is no shame you would not say 'no shame,'" she says. "You're a priest? Martin says you're a priest."

"No. I'm not."

"You studied . . ."

"I taught college."

"Not now?"

"No. I don't work."

"No shame in it." She smiles, that brown tooth, a gray-brown like a muddy ice puddle. There's a part of me that knows if she offers me a hand job right now, I'll say yes.

I turn to leave. The living room is empty, but the television whines.

THE BUS HOME SLOGS THROUGH TRAFFIC. I SIT WITH MY HEAD against the glass watching the city pass. Why did I choose to volunteer with hospice?

I told Carrie that it was a desire to serve. I told myself this too. And it's not completely untrue. But there was more. There was curiosity. A truly morbid curiosity.

I wanted to know what death looks like. What the smells and sounds of dying are.

The moment Miles was born I was struck by the fact of my own mortality. His new body wriggling pink on Carrie's chest—and I knew with an odd joy that he was here to eventually take my place on this planet. His birth clearly communicated my death.

In that first instant, I knew Miles was a miracle. I understand billions of babies have been born. I understand there is little as biologically mundane as birth. But can't the mundane be miraculous?

We brought our baby home. So small and real. I spent hours staring at his mewing mouth and the soft white fur that covered his pink skin and the red hairs on his oval head. His face moving through expressions, his limbs twitching out from his body.

Our house seemed different with him in it. Not just the toys and music boxes and onesies. It was the new scents and sounds and life. It was now home to a baby. Home to a family.

One morning, Miles woke with a cry just before dawn. I cradled him—small, warm body, less than a month in the world. I sang him Muppet songs while pouring myself a cup of coffee.

On our back porch his cries cooed away. I sat on our wooden rocking chair and he lay in the crook of my arm, his eyes moving through all kinds of mixed focus on trees and clouds and my face. It was autumn and the sharp air carried a soft humming.

It's easy to believe in the holy at dawn. I didn't say words or address God, but I knew sitting with Miles, watching him opening and closing his eyes and hands in the new autumn air, this was prayer.

The two oaks in the yard, the changing morning sky, the slight white steam from my cup. The world was enchanted. The soft hum touched it all. Nothing needed to be evidence of anything. All was as all was, and that was good.

I step off the bus into the downtown crowd. The middle-aged couple on a Segway tour, the hipsters sipping coffee or beer at the sidewalk tables outside the gourmet market, bluetooths and business suits. The sun sinks and the sky blurs orange.

I move south, away from the towering condos and new business buildings and toward the Congress Avenue Bridge. From the bridge, downtown burns in the last of the sunlight. Below me a lone rower slices through the lake, the water closing behind her like a fast-healing wound. Birds fly low over the waters, their reflections rippling from the wind of their own flight. A dog lumbers into the waters, cheered on by a laughing boy. The dog splashes after some geese too unthreatened to fly. They casually paddle away and the dog barks and the boy laughs and jumps and his mother stands near and the boy's laughter echoes up to me and over me and across all the waters.

You see? You see? I place my feet down on dead stone, but then beauty seizes me, kidnaps me. This sky. This air filling my lungs with each breath. This water clipping sunlight into countless diamond chips.

Something as subtle as scent pushes through me and I drown, for an instant, in the beauty. It's awe, as thoughtless as joy. Not my joy, but Joy. Joy that is and will be whether I am here to sense it or not. And for a breath, and for only a moment, I believe this Joy to be the true nature of all that is.

I would believe this world has no meaning, no soul. But I see this sky and taste this air and I held my child and I watched him cry his first breath. If the universe is nothing but rock and fire and the rules of physics, why does it hurt up and down and as far as it all stretches?

If I am being punished—God, Father, Mother, All—if I am being punished, let me see my sin. Please. Let me see that this somehow makes sense and the world is not just stone and death at its heart.

I WALK THE FEW REMAINING BLOCKS TO MY SHED. I MAKE MY WAY behind the darkened salon and stop. A thin line of light glows from under the door and the padlock dangles cut.

I step closer. Someone moves inside. It could be anyone.

I pick up a branch from the scattered debris fallen from the dying pecan tree and creep up the steps. The steps squeak and I pause just before the door, listening. I now see the branch is more of a stick, too thin to do much more than swat. I think about creeping back and grabbing something fiercer, but that would mean more squeaky steps. Instead I decide to act.

Bam. I push through the door screaming. Lyle squeals and lunges backward from my open mini fridge, sending a tray of ice up into the air, cubes flying like hail in a whirlwind.

"Jesus, Ollie," he says, one hand on the top of the mini fridge and the other on his heart. "You scared my colon clean."

"Lyle. What are you doing?"

"Recovering, now."

"Sorry." I lower my stick.

He regains his composure. "Close the door. You'll get mosquitoes." He returns to rooting through my fridge. "I snapped the lock for you," he says, his head in the fridge.

"I noticed that."

"You don't want to be crawling in and out of windows. You'll crack a rib and die."

"You don't die from cracked ribs."

"You do if it hurts to breathe and then you take shallow breaths all the time and you develop pneumonia." He straightens, clutching a container of cottage cheese. "I had a cousin die that way."

"Thanks." I sit on the edge of my bed.

"Got to look out for each other." He opens the cottage cheese, picks out a wet curdle and pops it in his mouth. "So, did you sell any body fluids today?"

"Fell off my to-do list."

"It's okay, I've got a better plan." He chomps a few more curdles. "Remember you said you wish you had as much sex as I have?"

"No, I don't remember saying that, Lyle."

"You've only had three women, right?"

"Yes, but—"

"I've got a solution to help you *and* make us money for the Yamal." Lyle tosses another curdle, it hits the side of his mouth and falls to the floor. He considers it for a moment, then returns his focus to me. "You, Ollie, will get paid to have sex with beautiful women."

He waits for my reaction. I have none to give.

"So many lonely, hot ladies, Ollie. We'll advertise on the net and set you up."

"For money?"

He drops into my only chair. "Think about it, Ollie. You're in good shape, got a PhD. We'll call you Doctor Ram, or something."

"I don't want to be a whore."

"That's a nasty word, Ollie. Lots of judgment in that word."

"I know. That's what I'm doing. I'm judging," I say. "Why don't you do it?"

"I can't. You know that. I've got Sue-Lee. She doesn't want to share unless she's there, you know what I mean," he says.

"No."

"I posted an ad on Craigslist."

"You did what?"

"We need the money. You need to get laid."

"Please go home. Please take that post off. Please."

"Are you frigid?"

"No."

"That could be something to work through."

"I'm not frigid. I just don't want to have sex for money, okay?"

Lyle studies me for a beat, then nods knowingly. "You don't think you're worth it."

"Jesus, Lyle."

"It's a self-esteem issue. I get it. Look, I've done the research. It's not a real high bar."

"Will you leave now?"

"Fine," he stands. "To the bold go the spoils."

He walks out, taking my cottage cheese with him.

There is money, enough to pay both our ways. But I won't touch it. It might as well be ash.

THE BLOND BOY AT SUNFLOWER DAYCARE LAUGHS AS HE KICKS OVER a pile of blocks. He falls and laughs.

As a baby Miles was, like all infants, a narcissist. It wasn't that he didn't care about the needs of others, he just couldn't comprehend them. The world outside his skin was emotionally zilch. In those first months, he cared for my wants or pains as much as I care for the pebbles of Pluto.

At fifteen months, Miles saw Carrie splash a ladle of boiling water on her chest. She cried out and placed a wet rag to the scald while I darted around looking for ointment. Miles watched our mayhem from the kitchen floor. Then, as I applied aloe vera to her blistering chest, Miles abandoned his toys, waddled to her side, and touched her back. His eyes carried new empathy—heavy and lifelong. *My god,* his eyes said, *it hurts to see you hurt.*

This blonde boy must shoulder that same weight for Carrie.

He leaps from the top of the Sunflower Daycare slide with a wild, holy cry.

"Archer," they call. "No jumping, Archer."

But he's already climbing back up.

"Free t-shirts, everyone," Charlie announces to the Agape Center crowd, pulling bright aqua-blue shirts from a box. They read: "NO MEANS NO. Spring Break, Austin, Texas."

John, a homeless man with the airs of a college professor, swears the police feed these kind of t-shirts into the homeless community. He calls them Targets. "Now they know who to harass. We're in uniform, for God's sake."

I sign up for a turn at the free computers and take a seat beside John. He takes notes in the margins of his Ken Wilbur book. I'm rereading *Our Journey In.*

At the same table sits a thin, mumbling woman, her body worn and bruised. She's surrounded by people I don't see, and she is in a constant argument with them. What are they telling her? Horrible things. Nagging. Every so often she screams back, sometimes throwing fists or chairs at her tormentors. Cops are called and she's dragged off to the Austin State Hospital. In three days, without fail, she's released back to the street, drugged into a temporary compliance.

Shelly walks by. She's pregnant again. She'll lose the baby—always does—either in pregnancy or days after it's born. Her mind is a child's, her body is raped on the street weekly. Even now.

In the corner Ashley sits with Joan. Joan, small and aged, shakes her head, her face wrinkling into itself. Every day she sits in her plastic chair, her eyes wide. She tells me her husband's body is laid out on the sidewalk. She tells me the city refuses to take his body. She tells me this nearly every day.

"Do you know how many people died on the streets last year?" John has placed his book down and has me fixed me in his gaze, his bushy gray eyebrows twitching. "Just in Austin," he continues. "On the streets and in the shelters. One hundred and forty-three."

"That's more than I thought," I say.

"Memorial service down by Lady Bird Lake. They read off all the names. Say a prayer or two. It's good." He knocks on his book likes it's a door. "Truth is they want us dead. Can't blame them. Clogging up the sidewalks and doorways. Look at her." He nods at the mumbling woman. "Be a lot easier just to sprinkle some rat poison in a soup kitchen Thanksgiving dinner. Clean the streets in one night." He runs a tongue over his teeth. "Be a helluva lot faster than the way they kill us now. Maybe kinder."

"How do they do it now?"

"Same way the Romans did with unwanted babies." He grins. "Leave them to the elements. Find a spot outside of town, leave the baby and walk away fast so you don't have to hear the crying." His eyebrows do a little jig. "Actually, we're worse. That baby dies in a day. It has to, all alone outside the city wall. But our babies are on the corners at traffic lights. We keep them barely alive with spare change. Minimum wage, same thing. Just enough to survive, not enough to live."

"Still got a bed at the Arch?"

"Nope. Staying in a friend's storage unit." He smiles. "Four walls and a roof."

I have two new emails. The first is a forward from Lyle. A note from none other than Dr. Jim Horner.

> **Dear Fellow Explorer,**
>   **Welcome and congratulations!**
>   You are one of an elite group of men and women who will venture forth into unexplored lands in the Yamal. Great adventures await us.

The entire itinerary is forthcoming plus a full list of all needed supplies.

Please note that a deposit of half your expedition is due as a down payment within six weeks of receiving this note.

Onward and Inward!

Dr. Jim Horner

The second email is from God:

Dear Oliver Bonds

I have your son here with me. He has some words for you. Being that I'm a loving God, I won't share them. But you can probably imagine.

Your Eternal Father,

God

"What are you up to?" Ashley stands behind me.

"An email from God," I say. "He writes me every few months. Been doing it for a few years now."

She nods, reading the address. "God@zipmail.com. Cute."

"How's Joan?" I ask.

"Crazy," she says with a shrug. "And off her meds."

"She's been here for years."

"Not surprised. She's not crazy enough to hurt people so she won't go to jail and she's not sane enough to seek help. She's stuck." She reaches and takes a piece of my popcorn. "She won't get off the streets."

"Sometimes she sings," I say. "Quietly, under her breath."

She looks at me quizzically, then back at my screen. "So what does God say?"

"Threats, mainly."

She purses her lips and leans over my shoulder and reads the note. Her hair touches my shoulder.

"You don't know who it is?" she asks, her eyes on the screen.

I shake my head. She smells like flowers.

She stands straight and frowns.

"Write him back and tell him to fuck off."

"That's what they taught you in grad school?"

She smiles, turning. "Oklahoma can change a girl."

I face my screen and stare at the email. Honestly, writing back had never occurred to me. She's right, I could tell God to fuck off, to stop writing. I put my fingers to the keys. I want to write. But my fingers don't move. They won't move.

Someone calls my name and I turn to see Lyle striding through the crowded room toward me.

"Thought I'd find you here. Did you get my email?" he asks. "Oh, thank God. Coffee."

He redirects himself to the vat of coffee and grabs a mug. I join him.

"Shouldn't you be asleep?" I ask.

He sips and speaks over the lip of the mug. "Crew boss called. They're short so I'm working a double. Going to pull some convention fat asses till sundown, then do the 6th Street crowd. We've got to make some scratch."

"Right. Scratch."

"Sir," Charlie waddles up trying to smile through a frown. "We need all neighbors to sign in."

"Oh, I'm not homeless," Lyle says. "I'm just underdressed."

"Charlie, this is a friend of mine."

"This coffee is outstanding," Lyle says as he refills his mug. "And it's free?"

"The grounds are donated," Charlie says. "We brew it here. But sir—"

"You should be charging for this," he says.

"That would kind of defeat the purpose," I say.

"Not to them," he gestures to the room. "But guys like me. Sell it for a buck." As he speaks, Lyle pulls a bike water bottle from his back pocket. "You'd make a hundred in an hour and you could get some decent creamer instead of this powder shit."

Lyle places the bottle under the spout and lets the coffee pour.

"Sir," Charlie says. "We need to save the coffee for the neighbors."

"You don't have brown sugar, do you?" Lyle asks.

"Sir, we need to ration the supplies for the neighbors. We operate on a small bu—"

"That's cool. Trying to cut back anyway." He sips from the open water bottle and glances at Charlie's nametag. "Hey, thanks for the help, Charlie, but I need to chat with Ollie here and it's kind of private. So . . ."

Charlie frowns at me. I shrug.

"If he stays, he has to sign in, okay?" Charlie says, and walks away flustered.

"I did some research on selling body fluids," Lyle says, pulling a folded piece of paper from his pocket. "Lists all the places in town you can sell blood, plasma, and semen."

"Ten thousand dollars worth?"

"Inch by inch, Ollie."

"Lyle," I say, reading through the lists of clinics and donation centers. "I don't think I can give blood. I was in prison."

"For like a day." Lyle squirts the coffee into his mouth, then smiles. "Man, I've got to stop in here more often."

THE SKY IS CLEAR AS I WALK FROM AGAPE. SIXTH STREET IS A HARSH sight in the daylight. Deserted and strange, the bar signs and drink specials as gaudy as a Christmas tree come January. There's something corpse-like about the block—or perhaps mannequin-like. It was only a trick of light that made this place seem alive.

"Buy me a drink?" Ashley says. She's walking beside me pulling on her jacket.

"Hi," I say, blinking too many times. "Done for the day?"

"Nothing but paperwork. I cut out a little early. Miriam was out so I told Charlie I had a doctor's appointment. Said it was a lady issue. That was enough for him to wish me gone. He has a paralyzing fear of fallopian tubes and related body parts." She maneuvers her back, whipping the jacket into place over her shoulders. "So, buy me a drink?"

"I don't drink."

"I do," she says, keeping pace with me. "Buy me one?"

"I don't have any money."

"I'll lend you some."

"Why don't you just buy your own drink?" I ask.

"It's eleven in the morning. If I'm buying drinks at this hour, I've got a problem." She touches my elbow and smiles. "So, buy me a drink?"

We find a beer-stink bar that looks surprised to be awake. She drinks whiskey on the rocks. I order water.

"I thought you'd write."

"I thought it best not to." I sip my water. And for a moment it is quiet. But it's a quiet I recognize and I know what she will say before she says it.

"Can I ask you what happened?"

"I think you may know."

Quiet.

"I thought you'd rather tell me," she says.

"Why did you think that?"

"We used to talk."

"Sure," I say.

"So, tell me."

"Mother said if you can't say anything nice, don't say anything at all."

"Do you talk to anybody?" she asks.

"I have two friends," I say. "One is dying and the other is a liar."

"Beggars can't be choosers."

"Mother said that, too."

She smiles and lifts her glass. "You could have written me. Talked to me." She takes a sip. "The police called me. They called me in Bolivia."

I nod. I figured they would have.

"My father was so mad. He made me come home. Hired this crazy lawyer . . ." She takes a swallow of her drink and looks at me. "You don't want to tell me what happened?"

"I'm taking a trip to the center of the earth," I say. "Into the hollow earth."

She pauses, trying to read me. "What's the hollow earth?"

"It's the theory that the earth is hollow and possibly inhabited."

"But it's not."

I shrug. "There's a lot of science that says otherwise," I say. "1692. Sir Halley, of Halley's Comet, publishes a paper titled *An Account of the Cause of the Change of Variation of the Magnetical Needle with a Hypothesis of the Structure of the Internal Parts of the Earth*. He was the first modern scientist to acknowledge that the earth is hollow."

"What about gravity?" she says. "I mean, wouldn't a hollow planet just collapse? All the heaviest stuff moving to the center?"

"Ever ride one of those carnival rides? The kind that spins and pins you to the wall? Earth spins. The force throws matter outwards. Our gravity is in the crust. So dig down deep enough and you'll come out on the inner surface."

"And this is where you're going? You're digging a hole to the center of the earth?"

"The holes are already there. Hidden all over in caves and mineshafts. Probably even a few in Texas. But the biggest are near the South and North Pole. Symmes Holes. Hundreds of miles wide. Maybe a thousand."

"Is this where Santa lives?"

I close my mouth.

"I'm sorry," she says. "I've never heard any of this before."

"The cover-up has been extensive."

She nods as she studies me.

"Are you living on the street?" she asks.

"I have a place."

"Are you on any medication?"

"Is this a drink or admittance exam?"

"I'm just trying to figure out what happened," she says.

"You know what happened."

She chews her cheek and leans back. "So what's inside a hollow earth?" she asks.

I shrug. "We live on the outside skin of a balloon. Maybe others live on the inside of the skin. Maybe it's full of dinosaurs and giants or some advanced race or Nazis."

"Nazis?"

"Hitler believed in the hollow earth, that's documented. At least twice during the war, he sent expositions to the North Pole. Some people speculate that a Nazi base in Neuschwabenland was actually an entry into the hollow earth and it was Hitler's escape plan. Some think he's there now, hiding out with a few dedicated followers."

"He'd be dead by now," she says.

"Not if the inner sun prolongs life, as most believe."

"When you say *most* . . ."

"Most hollow earthers."

"Oh," she says, her nod light and condescending. "And you believe all this? Hollow earth, inner sun, Nazis?"

"The Nazi idea is just a theory."

She stares at me, waiting. I tap the table. She keeps watching me for a long quiet moment.

"Those emails . . ." I begin. "The notes signed from God . . . I can't picture who it is."

"It could be anyone," she says. "Some troll read about you in the news and has a hard-on for torture."

"I mean, I can't imagine a person. I try—some kid in a basement or something—but no image sticks." I pause. "Do you know the second commandment?"

"No graven images, right?"

"'*Thou shall not make unto thee any graven image, or any likeness of any thing that is in heaven above.*' You're not allowed to picture the divine." I shake my head. "If I could imagine a person I could dismiss it. But I can't. I just have these messages from nowhere. And nowhere is everywhere."

"Just like God," she says.

"How can you argue with what you cannot comprehend?"

"Dr. Bonds, God is not sending you emails."

"Did you know that same verse, Exodus 20:4, tells us we're also forbidden to make images of all that '*is in the earth beneath.*'? It's true, '*in the earth beneath.*' The hollow earth. I'm breaking this commandant all the time. I'm crafting image after image of earth beneath. But I don't hold on to any one image for very long. I imagine crystal cities and singing giants. I imagine flesh-eating insects the size of horses. I imagine oceans of souls swirling. Anything is possible."

"In a lecture you said human beings will believe almost anything."

"I said human beings have the *capacity* to believe almost anything."

She smiles and drains her drink. "Look at us, Dr. Bonds. It's like we're back at school."

"My tits hurt, Ollie!" Carrie said, stepping away.

"I'll avoid them."

"Hell yeah, you'll avoid them." We laughed. But it was a tight, mean mirth from both of us.

Carrie and I had made love twice since his birth.

Miles was over a year old—first steps and new words. But days had no rest, no pause, and nights were spurts of sleep interrupted by panic yells. We were ragged with sleeplessness, both of us sensitive as broken teeth.

"Do you know how long it's been since I've slept more than three consecutive hours, Oliver?"

"I know, I know."

"I feel crazy, Oliver. Really crazy."

We argued in ways we never had—stone-sharp words and boiling silences. I felt thick shame on many of those days, understanding this should be the happiest time of my life, but finding myself overwhelmed and, at times, resentful.

Carrie's sister suggested the Cry-it-Out Method. So we bought a book (there was always a book) and chose the first week of winter break to teach the baby how to sleep.

The book laid out a three-day plan. First night the baby cries and you go into the nursery, you touch his back, but you don't pick him up. When he cries again, you wait ten minutes before going in to him and again touch his back. Next time you wait fifteen minutes. Night two, you don't go in at all. He cries. You wait. He cries. We were told this led to self-soothing.

The urge—animal deep—is go and gather your child. To hold him. But we followed the book. We always followed a book. It was hellish, but it was effective. Night three, no tears.

Strange, but the next few nights I woke to no cries and lay in the silence. No more night vigils. Rocking him, pacing to the rhythm of Iron & Wine ballads. Miles mewing, chewing on my T-shirt.

At times I found myself missing the cries and cursing the sleep.

And even as Miles slept, Carrie and I hardly touched.

Her desire was gone. A chemical change. This was as incomprehensible to me as losing the desire to eat. Skipping a meal—or several—I could understand. But to lose the sensation of hunger? We had enjoyed so many meals together. And how good had it been to find we were almost always hungry at the same time?

I was starving. Carrie had no appetite at all.

"Come on, Carrie," I said. "I just feel it would bring us closer."

"You sound like a sixteen-year-old begging for a hand job."

"A hand job would be nice."

"You've got a hand," she said. "Use it."

"It's been four months."

"You're counting!"

"I'm aware."

"Jesus, you have a punch card or something?"

I *felt* like a sixteen-year-old, the same bubbling frustration, the same conniving, clumsy attempts at seduction. How many mornings did I snuggle to her and have her roll away? How many nights did I touch her back as we stood in the kitchen only to have her flinch?

Her body had been given over. The entry point had become an exit route. Her breasts, food processors. Her body was for a baby, not for me. I was jealous. Jealous of my infant son. Jealous of the unquestioning adoration she poured on him.

It was not just the sex I missed. I missed her. I missed her horribly. Missed a shared bottle of wine and late breakfasts and mid-day movies. And doing nothing. Being in the same space with time to do nothing. I missed her. I missed that life. And I pouted.

I was afraid. Afraid she'd given up and joined this other tribe—the neutered, bland, minivan tribe. I feared that soon, like a beaten dog, I'd stop pursuing her, stop chasing what I couldn't have, stop even wanting it. Feared I'd lose my sex and with it my youth.

I had a wonderful new baby. I was grateful. I knew Carrie and I were in the weeds and compassion and patience marked the way forward. There was that spiteful sixteen-year-old in my head frustrated as hell he wasn't getting laid.

Ashley took my Wisdom Literature course that semester—three seats in, two rows back.

SHE WAS JUST ANOTHER STUDENT. A LITTLE MORE ATTENTIVE THAN the yawning store-bought blondes and grade-hungry business majors who populated my classes. A little sadder, perhaps. A little more sarcastic. She dressed in browns and black, a mature air, if a bit forced. Pale legs, like yogurt. In colder weather she'd splotch red, yogurt with raspberries. She wore the same slight scent as she does today—cut flowers.

Ashley did not flirt. I had female students who did—the same crafted flirt they had practiced on high school coaches and friends' fathers. A playful, girlish sexuality asking for treats and special treatment. Ashley did none of this.

But she did return to my office hours. We discussed her plans to earn a masters and a PhD in religious studies, we covered other subjects in the class—Book of Ecclesiastes, gnostic gospels, Tao Te Ching. She told me about her family—a father she despised and a sister she hardly saw. But eventually we always came back to Job.

"Does Job believe in heaven?" She referred to Job in the present, the grammatically proper way to refer to a character in fiction as opposed to a historical figure. That was my influence. "There's all that stuff about how brief life is. How death lasts forever. But there's Sheol. Sheol is like heaven, right?"

"Sheol is death," I said. "Not unlike the Greek's Hades. It's not really an afterlife, it's more a depiction of how these ancients view non-life. Job calls it, 'The black, disordered land where darkness is the only light.'"

"So no Hallmark cards saying 'Sorry for your loss. Your loved one is in a better place'?"

"I doubt there was much of a market."

"My mother loved saying that. Anyone—any*thing* died. Your goldfish is in a better place. So very lucky to die." She bit at her thumbnail. "So Sheol . . . Everyone goes there?"

"Everyone."

"Except God."

"It's the place you go when God forgets your name."

When I spoke of belief from a book or a tradition, I didn't qualify it with "According to Job" or "The Romans believed." I spoke of each religion as my own. Temporarily claiming its beliefs, at least grammatically.

I can be quoted as saying:

"God tolerates humanity, but just barely."

"We've all been reborn countless times. And will continue to be until we attain liberation."

"And a horn will be blown loud enough to be heard the whole world over, and the Chosen will be swept up to meet Jesus in the sky."

This tendency to slip in and out of religious personas through one lecture simultaneously entertained and baffled my students. They made a game of trying to pin down what I actually believed. They'd quiz me, try and snag me in a trap, like the Pharisees questioning Jesus on paying taxes.

I was arrogantly objective, convinced that only a non-believer may study what others believe. I did my best to be neutral and non-judgmental. But in truth, I judged anyone who wasn't the same kind of neutral as me.

If intensely pressed—usually by a wide-eyed, C.S. Lewis-quoting evangelical with an unquenchable mission to convert their hellbound professors—I'd confess that my family attended St. Christopher's Episcopalian church. This relaxed them. But I added that I refused to sign any statement of belief. I wasn't a believer.

Part of this was based on my own prejudice against defining members of a tradition as *believers*. The concept that our beliefs define us as opposed to our actions is a modern western view I found narrowing.

But more than that, I believed I believed nothing.

It wasn't true.

I believed, without ever saying it, that the world was basically good. I believed moral behavior was rewarded by the world. I believed cruelty to be its own kind of punishment. And though I never would have admitted it to anyone, least of all myself, I believed that the most horrible things don't really happen.

I saw the photos of typhoons drowning entire villages or genocidal wars. Monthly I tithed to charities aiming to end modern slavery or encourage basic health care in poorer nations. But in some deep secret way, I didn't *believe* in these tragedies. They were distant, unreal, fantastic. Or, worse, I believed I simply didn't see the bigger picture, the vague grander scheme that explained these tragedies.

I had one over-arching belief, so basic to my life that I never felt the need to distinguish it as a belief any more than a person would count the sun's heat as an article of faith. I believed the world made sense.

As the weeks rolled by, Ashley's conversation grew more sophisticated, her thinking sharper. The class was now discussing the feminine portrayal of wisdom in Proverbs. Ashley was still on Job.

"So basically theodicy comes down to this," she said one afternoon. "God is either all-powerful but not all-loving—he could help us, but won't. Or God's all-loving, but not all-powerful. He'd rather us not suffer, but there's nothing he can do about it. Sadistic or weak, take your pick."

"That's the Epicurean paradox," I said, a tad smugly. I was often a tad smug in my office. "But there's another option. Perhaps suffering is there to teach us something."

"Redemptive suffering," she said, her forehead frowning. "You mentioned that in class."

"It's perhaps our culture's greatest myth." I liked that statement. I had said it often "It's in every Hollywood movie. The hero has to suffer before he wins the day. And, of course, Christian theology is built on the idea that the God-Man's suffering redeems the world."

"It's the same bullshit Job's friends feed him." She leaned back, propping a foot on the edge of my desk. Her leg, I noticed, was defined, firm, and pale as winter. "Suffering comes straight from God—either to punish us or teach or redeem us. Suffering serves a purpose. It's bullshit."

"In *Man's Search for Meaning*, Frankl says—"

"I know. I know," she said, rolling her eyes. "The world is meaningless so we must invent our own meaning."

Her foot on my desk, her eyes rolling like some teen told to turn down the stereo, but her mind crafting arguments and questions.

"More bullshit," she said. "Instead of inventing meaning, maybe we just to need to come to terms with meaninglessness."

I smiled. "You are going to love grad school."

She chuckled and the edge of her cheekbones blushed pink.

I'd all but promised her admission to the University of Texas Masters program for the following Fall. In time, I'd oversee her thesis, perhaps her dissertation. We had years ahead of us.

I WATCH FROM THE SIDEWALK AS THE BLONDE BOY CRAWLS ON TOP OF the monkey bars. His face shines. The teacher doesn't see him. She's with a child in the sandbox. Besides me, a little girl is the only other witness of his feat. She grins wildly at him, clapping her hands. He's won her heart for life.

His right hand slips. I call out, seeing what will happen. The teacher looks up as he falls, hitting the ground with a thud.

"Archer!" I call.

The teacher scoops him up, hushing his tears. She glares at me, then turns to the building.

THE WHOLE AGAPE CENTER SMELLS OF POPCORN. THEY COOK UP A batch up every Friday and play a rented DVD in the gym.

When I volunteered a retired actuary named Daniel made the popcorn. He would make one batch with double the artificially flavored butter oil. The popcorn came out wet and delicious. The neighbors loved it. "Ha," Daniel would call out as he stepped from the kitchen with a tray of bagged popcorn, the paper already transparent from the oil. "Come and get it." And they would. They'd rush to it. "Popcorn crack," he'd say to me.

Davis spills sweetener. He's twenty or so, lives at home with his parents but comes to Agape for breakfast at least twice a week. Half his body doesn't work and the left side of his face swells like a rotten fruit. Davis idolizes Elvis. Every month or so he dyes his blond reedy hair jet black and twists his body, hubbubbing at the neighbors and high school youth groupers who volunteer on their school breaks.

Davis tells me he's engaged. The mother-in-law-to-be doesn't approve, but he's engaged. Elvis's mother-in-law-to-be hated him too. But Elvis didn't care. Elvis did what he wanted to do.

As Davis chronicles Elvis's romantic accomplishments, a man rushes up to us, his two middle bottom teeth missing. His eyes ice blue and wide. "I can't stay. Wish I could. I can't stay. I'm off to lunch. You know, I have nine years of college. I have a masters. I could fix that computer, if it ever breaks. I can. I fixed one for the Baptists. And I play. Cello, piano, bass. I picked up a bass and played. People said, my god, look how you play? Been doing it for thirty years! I can tune that." He points to the old piano against the wall. "I can tune that, easy. I did that for the Baptists, too. I tuned it and they said, my God that plays good. And I said yeah. I have perfect pitch. Ahhhh. That's B- flat. I know. I've got perfect pitch. But I still want to improve myself. Still want to further my education. Can't have enough education. But I can't stay. Wish I could."

Ben comes in from outside, his face swelling around his ping-pong eyes. From the cheekbone up, his face is a red wound bruising purple and yellow.

"What happened?" I ask.

"Gravity," he says.

As I wait for the computer, I pick up a water-logged King James Bible from the window sill. I flip through the wrinkled pages. Blue ink handwriting catches my eye. A scrawled sentence at the top of a page of Deuteronomy.

"And the Lord said, 'Bitch, give me head.'"

Charlie tells me I have twenty minutes on the computer. I have two new emails. Lyle has forwarded an email from Dr. Jim Horner with a single line note "ASKING FOR AN EXTENSION!!!"

Fellow Explorer, Welcome.

The truth awaits us!

We will depart from Moscow, Russia on June 26th. Please note: you will need to provide your own travel arrangements to and from Moscow.

JUNE 26-27: Arrive in Moscow. Spend the rest of the day sightseeing Moscow.

JUNE 27: Take a morning flight to Murmansk, Russia. Here we will board the Russian Icebreaker Yamal.

JUNE 28th–JULY 2nd: On the journey to the North Pole, we will compare notes and prepare for the journey within.

JULY 3rd–5th: Reach the North Polar Symmes opening, which we calculate to be in the vicinity of 84.4 N Latitude, 141 E. Longitude. With any luck, we will actually cross into the hollow earth on America's Independence Day!

JULY 6th–8th: We will continue our exploration and video chronicling of our discoveries. It is our hope to reach the theoretical city of Jehu.

JULY 9th–11th: After making diplomatic contact with the people within, we will return via the North Pole Symmes opening.

JULY 12th–16th: We sail back to Murmansk examining and correlating our collected data.

JULY 17th: Return from Murmansk to Moscow.

Please remember that the down payment for your spot on the Yamal is due by this month's end.

Looking forward to our adventure!
Dr. Jim Horner

(Note. If we are prevented from entering the North Polar Symmes opening by environmental or governmental obstacles, we will return to Murmansk via the New Siberian Islands to visit skeleton remains of exotic animals thought to originate from Inner Earth)

The next email is from god@zipmail.com.

> **Dear Oliver**
> **I dare you to take justice into your own hands. You know what you deserve. Now do it.**
> **God, your Eternal Father**

I read it over and over. Then I hit reply.

> **God—**

First, that's all I can manage. I stare at that word and the blank white below.

> **God—**

Maybe that's all I'll write. Then Charlie tells me I have only two minutes left on the computer. I type:

> **God—**
> **I will if You will.**
> **Oliver**

I press send.

When I leave an hour later Davis is singing "Heartbreak Hotel" to a cheering few. He's swinging his hips, spilling his popcorn into their coffee and lemonade.

IT WAS THE LAST OFFICIAL DAY OF THE FALL SEMESTER. I GRADED THE final essays in my university office. Outside, the near empty campus was grey dark, the weather turning to a mild winter chill.

Miles was a just over a year old that December. I wanted him to have an ideal Christmas. I wanted him to have a stocking and a tree and sit on Santa's lap.

But even these thoughts left me tired. I hated how tired I was. I wanted to want my life more than I did. The encroaching three-week vacation sat in my belly like indigestible lunch. A slight dread of the unscheduled days, the sexless bed, and the lack of a job to disappear into.

As I sat, the ungraded essays piled before me and the afternoon darkening out my window, a voice whispered my name. "Dr. Bonds?"

Ashley smiled, her wind-blushed face peeking through my half-open door. She came in carrying two coffees. "Still doing office hours?"

She lowered herself into the chair.

"Ready for graduation?"

"Robed and ready." She handed me the coffee.

"It's not necessary," I said. "You've got your 4.0"

She smiled, blushing. Or maybe that was just the cold. She chewed her cheek. I watched her dimple sink and reappear.

"What's on your mind, Ashley?"

"Explain God's answer," she said quickly, as if the idea had just occurred to her. "Job demands a trial. God shows up in a tornado—"

"A whirlwind, yes."

"And brags about how big and all-knowing divinity is. How God wrestles sea monsters and controls the stars. What the hell is that all about? It's nonsensical."

"Awe, I suppose."

"Awe." She stood and walked to my shelves, mindlessly scanning the titles as she spoke.

"God gives Job a glimpse of it all. The massive wonder of creation," I said. "He doesn't apologize. He doesn't comfort. He only points to how awesome the universe is. The incomprehensible complexity and scale of it all."

"Bragging," she said, crossing her arms and jutting out her hip. Bored, and angry for being bored.

"That's an anthropomorphic slant."

"You're the one using the masculine pronoun."

"Okay." I chuckle. "Let's say God represents the universe here. Job cries out that the universe is unjust. The universe doesn't even address the charges. Just blazes. The universe is saying it doesn't have to explain itself, it's just awesome. As in inspiring reverence, even terror. I mean, we don't ask the stars to be *good* or the Grand Canyon to be *just.*"

"So God is saying, 'I am what I am and that's all that I am.'"

"That's what He told Moses. 'I am who I am'," I said. "Or what *She* told Moses."

Ashley laughed through her nose.

"What about love?"

"What about it?"

Her eyes stayed on mine. "Love. Isn't God supposed to love us?"

"Maybe Job is telling us love looks different than we thought. Perhaps divine love is incomprehensible."

"That's horseshit. You know that, right?"

I nod, smiling. But she doesn't. The play seemed to drain from the conversation. And I remembered—*mother was a suicide.*

"So in the end, God can't answer Job. Not really." Her eyes are dark.

"Job gets no answer," I say. "But he gets to see God."

"And that's enough?"

"For Job it is."

"I'm not going to grad school, Dr. Bonds."

I twisted in my chair. "Not going to grad school? But you're already accepted. You're—"

"I'm going to Bolivia."

"The country?" I asked, stupidly.

"Volunteering with the Quakers. They've got a clean water initiative. I applied a month ago."

"Quakers?" All I seemed to be capable of doing was repeating her statements as questions. "You're a Quaker now?"

"I like them. They don't talk so much. I'm tired of talking. And grad school would just be more talking." She walked to the front of my desk, arms open. "You want to know how to answer suffering? Do something. I don't *do* anything." She picked up her backpack and turned to the door. "I should get going."

I stood up. "Have I offended you in some way, Ashley?"

She turned, surprised, then shook her head.

"No," she said. "It's not that."

I started to round my desk, but she was already gone.

That's when I knew I'd gone too far. I felt stupid, old. What kind of murky fantasies had I been running through? Nothing projected on the forefront of my thinking, but in the basement of my thinking. Vague ideas of her body, her hands.

Damn it. As if she was thinking of me as anything more than a teacher. I was not even forty and so damn old. A joke.

Was I planning on cheating on Carrie? I had no conscious ambitions. But looking honestly, and at that moment I was looking honestly, I wanted that girl. I wanted it to happen. So it was good that she'd left. That I wouldn't see her again. Good for me and my marriage and my family. So what was this regret?

I sat for minutes staring into nothing and feeling a weird shame and embarrassment and, more than anything, frustration. Frustration at my juvenile desires, my water-soup soul.

The door opened again and she came back, her cheeks pink.

Cradled in her palms she held an ink-black bird. "I wasn't sure what to do."

She placed the thing on my desk. I stood, stepping back and instinctively hiding my hands behind my back.

"It's a grackle," I said. "It's a dead grackle."

"I was just outside the doors, and it flew straight into the front windows. Can you help it?"

Its neck was bent awkwardly, it's wings limp. "It's dead."

"Poor thing," she said. I watched her, watched her eyes shine. Those same eyes that only minutes ago smoldered cold. She stroked the bird's oily feathers.

"They're not nice birds, Ashley," I said, crossing my arms. "One less grackle is no real trage— Jesus!"

A wing flapped.

"It's alive!" Ashley yelped.

In response the bird cried a single sharp sound filled with as much confusion and panic as one note can hold.

"Help it!" She looked at me wildly.

"Okay. I'll call— God damn!" It was trying to fly, both wings slapping against the desk, knocking a cup of pens over.

"Maybe it just needs a minute," Ashley said, reaching out an open palm to the bird. "Poor thing."

Just before she touched it, the bird took flight, zipping up and slamming against the ceiling of my office. It skittered along the ceiling to a corner, its wings beating furiously.

"Open a window," Ashley called out.

I turned to the window. I had never once opened it. Never once thought how to open it.

The bird abandoned the corner and searched for some escape. It alternately flapped and fell, making an uneven wave across the room, balancing for a moment on a book shelf, file cabinet, the frame of my PhD degree and scanning the room with twitchy glances for an instant before again launching into a panicked flight. Ashley rushed after it like a child chasing the tail of a kite.

The sound was ghastly, the rustling of wings against walls and panicked caws. Ashley laughed as she hounded the thing—cooing and laughing. But this wasn't funny. This was horrible.

I climbed onto my desk chair to get to the metal latch halfway up the pane. The grackle buzzed my head, feathers in my face. "Jesus, fuck!"

I shoved against the window. It gave way and I caught myself against the closed half, glimpsing the two-story fall.

Ashley flapped her hands at the bird, trying to usher it toward the window. The bird flew up and perched on the top of my doorframe. It examined me standing by the open window and Ashley smiling and waving at it. Its black eyes focused on the trees and sky outside, and it seemed to nod. It shot toward the window and smacked into the unopened half of the pane.

A thin, single six-inch crack appeared in the glass and the bird fell with a muffled thud on my office floor.

Standing on my chair, I looked down on it. Purple-black, twitching, and so far below me. *Are not two sparrows sold for a penny? And not one of them shall fall on the ground without your Father.*

Ashley rushed to it, gently cupping her hands under it and lifting it to my desk.

"No, no," she breathed.

I climbed down and stood beside her. The bird jerked its head about, extended its wings and crapped on my desk.

"Poor thing," she said. "It's dying."

It was convulsing, its twitching body flapping uselessly, moving like a feathered black crab over my ungraded essays. A dry, frantic sound—the spasm of a paper heart.

I turned from the bird and watched Ashley. Her eyes wide, her cheeks red, her lips full. She did not look as horrified as I felt. Quite the contrary. She looked, for lack of a better word, aroused. That was it. She was thrilled, awake, flushed.

"It's gone," she said, looking up at me, her face glowing, her breath fast. With no warning, she leaned across the corner of the desk and kissed my dry lips.

She pulled back, surprised at her actions. Then quickly hugged me, moaning a breath in my ear. She pushed away and stood looking at me for an instant. Grabbing her bag, she rushed from the office, leaving me standing brain-drunk with a broken window and a dead bird.

SAM THROWS OPEN THE DOOR AND GRINS. "HEY, IT'S THE PREACHER." He turns and heads to the kitchen. "Got a new bit in the routine you should hear."

I step inside. "Is Martin here?"

"He's sleeping, I think." As he talks he takes a slice of cheese from the fridge and lays it atop a single serving basket of Sonic tater tots. "So much trash in town. Right? Trash everywhere."

I nod. I think I'm supposed to. He puts the cheese and tots in the microwave oven.

"So I got a new job picking up trash," he says with a half shrug. "It's easy. I stroll 6th Street with my dick hanging out."

He grins.

I blink.

He nods.

I tell my mouth to smile, but I can't say what my mouth does. I doubt it smiles.

Bing. The tater tots are done.

"You get the joke, man. I'm picking up trash. Like, sluts. That kind of trash. And I'm doing it with my dick."

"Oh, yeah, yeah. I see now."

He shakes his head, angry.

"It's fucking funny if you had a sense of humor." He stabs a cheesy tot with a plastic fork.

"That's a good joke," I say.

He's got a mouthful of tater tots and cheese and he's chewing past the heat. His brow burrows down into the bridge of his nose. Then he turns and walks to the TV. A history of hurricanes on the Weather Channel.

I take my cue and walk back to Martin's room. The door is closed, a picture of a yellow Lotus taped to the door. From the other side the Steve Miller Band plays on some alarm clock radio. I knock lightly.

"Yeap," comes Martin's drawl.

"It's Oliver."

"Hey!" I can hear him smiling through the door. Lots of his words smile. "Open her up. Open her up."

The smoke in Martin's room overwhelms the smell of tots. A few strands of sunlight come through the blinds of the small, high window in the room. Martin pushes himself up from his easy chair and takes me into a hug. He's thinner than even a week ago. His body unsteady, but his hug is sure. He lowers himself back down. A can of tobacco and a pack of rolling papers lay on the table.

"Hot damn, Ollie! Good to see you."

Martin has a green-blue bruise on the side of his face.

"What happened?" I ask, touching my own face.

"Oh, you know. Nothing." He glances over my shoulder toward the living room. I close the door.

"What happened?"

I sit on the edge of his bed as he adjusts himself in the chair. He's small in the leather recliner, like a boy in his father's study.

"Nothing, really." He shakes his head. "We had a barbeque. Had some people over. Things got a little crazy." He smiles. "I had to have a talk with Sam. Talk it out."

"Your face and neck are bruised."

"I bruise pretty easy these days thanks to that goddamn chemo. I told him we got to straighten things up, we have to clean house. Keep things in order. I don't mind the girls. But no more parties. He got a little mad, but he heard me. Heard that we have to get these folks in line so we can keep this place. They raided two doors down last week. Dragged off a whole crew. He heard me."

"He hit you?"

"We got into a scuffle." He begins rolling another cigarette. "You should see him."

"I did. He looks fine."

"Well, he's got all those tats. Hard to see the scars."

He clears his throat for a full ten seconds, a slow gurgle like he's dragging his soul up through his throat. He swishes the load from cheek to cheek, then empties the mouthful into a tissue. I shouldn't look, but I do. The swampy green through the tissue white, like a wet goblin in a wedding dress.

"How are you feeling, Martin," I ask.

"Me?" He sniffles and uses the edges of the tissue to dab his nose. "Good. Really good. Better, even. Truth is I think I might beat this shit."

Taking aim, he tosses the tissue to a small trashcan in the corner. It flies heavy, like he'd coughed pennies into it. It hits the rim and falls to the floor.

"Damn," he says. Then looks to me. "Can you get that?"

I hesitate a moment, then stand and step toward the trashcan.

"Shit, Ollie," Martin laughs. "I'm joking. God damn."

"I've been told I don't have much of a sense of humor."

"You don't laugh much, that's true." He coughs into his fist. "You should try. It's good for you."

I nod.

"You miss your boy," he says.

I nod again and pick up his one golf club.

"You never talk about him."

"The words don't work," I say. "And I don't like people's faces when they hear."

"How's the whole hollow earth trip shaping up?" he asks.

"A little short on money."

"Expensive?" he asks.

"Very," I say, swinging the club.

Martin is silent for a beat, a half smile on his thin face. "Ollie, you really believe all that?"

I look at him.

"I mean, enough to take boat to the coldest place on earth to look for a hole?"

I shrug.

"Come on, Ollie."

I stop. I sit back on the edge of his bed and think a beat.

"Why do you want to get the Cadillac running?" I ask.

He frowns and leans back. "That's easy, I like to drive." He smiles a bit. "Used to just drive around west of town, out in the hills. Get a little lost." He gives a full grin. "It's fun."

"That's it," I say, tapping the club to the floor. "Honestly, Martin, hollow earth is the only fun I have."

I leave Martin's room an hour later. As I close his bedroom door, a lanky man steps from Sam's room and quickly heads out the front door. He turns as he walks out the front, flipping his chin in commiseration.

"Mr. Oliver," Laika says from Sam's room. The door is still ajar. "Can you come here to me?"

I look at the door—off white paint with greasy marks where a hundred hands have pressed. I step in. She's still in bed, bare white shoulders.

"I have to dress. They always want to start with me dressed." She stands, her nakedness as surprising as floating milk. But she's not displaying herself for me. She's moving to her clothes and leaning over for underwear. There is no sex in her nakedness. I notice her thick bush and glance away.

When was a woman nude before me without sex? An unguarded nudity—a fact rather than a demonstration or invitation. My wife, I suppose. College lovers and I never reached such intimacy.

"You are Martin's friend, yes? You are not here only because of the church."

"No," I say. "I was a hospice volunteer. That's how we met."

"Hospice." She pulls on a loose dress and faces me. "I don't know hospice."

"Helping people die."

She frowns. "People need help?"

"So they don't die alone," I say. It doesn't sound right. "Hospice helps people die well."

"People can die well." She hums and I'm not sure if she's asked a question or stated an opinion. "I've seen someone not die well."

"Who?" I ask.

"I have someone coming soon and there is something I wanted to talk to you about."

"Was it one of your parents?"

She sits on the bed and sighs through her nose. "My grandmother did not die well," she says, nodding. "She died slow and very angry. She was difficult."

"That happens."

"I was young. Nine, I think." She pulls on her shoes. They strap around her ankle. "I was alone with her when she died. I had to stay with the body. She turned yellow like spoiled cream." She looks up at me. "You've seen many dead people, I presume."

"Two," I say.

"That is not many."

"A lot of hospice clients just want a ride to the grocery store or someone to watch TV with."

"My clients too."

I lean against the wall. "I was ready for long philosophical conversations about faith and mortality. With all my studies I thought I'd be perfect, you know. And I'm not a horrible listener. But my first assigned case was a nearly non-verbal mentally retarded man."

"Non-verbal?"

"He could hardly speak," I say. "He loved milk shakes. So that's all we did. We'd go to the mall or McDonald's and have a milk shake. And he kept getting smaller. His mother called me one day and said he couldn't leave the house anymore. I went over and his mother met me at the door. She was a small Mexican woman. Didn't speak much English."

"Like me," she says.

"Your English is very good."

She smiles.

"He was in bed, just barely there, taking these shallow, rattling breaths. And I knew I had to be calm. In training they had warned us against panicking and calling 911. I called the hospice on-call doctor and he casually told me I was right, the man was about to die."

"Did you tell the mother?"

"She knew. She kept cleaning his face. Kept saying she had cared for him for thirty-two years. She was kind of manic. She tried to get him to drink some juice and spilled a little on his shirt. And when she ran to get a new one he looked at me with these questions and I didn't know what to say, so I said he was doing exactly what he should be doing, He was doing everything right."

"He was dying well?"

"He was dying. His body going through the textbook stages." I hide my hands in my pockets. "She wanted to change his shirt. I said he was fine, better not to move him, but she had to. He was too weak to sit up, so I held him. He was light, just empty. It was like holding a bird. She took his shirt off and sponged his chest like he was a baby. I'm sure just like she did when he was baby. Then she pat dried him with a towel and hushed him. She pulled a new shirt over his body and we lowered him back. His face cringed, I remember, like he'd pulled a muscle. Then he died. He died as we lay him down."

"She was a good mother."

"I guess that bath only sped things up, though."

"There's better things than time," she says.

I look at her. She studies her chipped fingernails.

"Why did you leave Russia? I ask.

"I have a daughter," she says, picking at a hangnail. "And a husband." She looks up, studying my face for a reaction. I don't give her one. For an instant her closed mouth stretches out—not a smile, not a frown, just a line. "I came here with a work visa and had a job with computers. The plan was for me to make lots of money and for them to someday come here as well." She returns to the hangnail. "But the job stopped and the visa stopped and I was still here." The hangnail comes free. She rubs it between her thumb and forefinger. "I send money back to Russia and I don't tell them what I do."

"How old is she?" I ask. "Your daughter."

She lifts her head and frowns. "Listen." She stands. "I should tell you while I can. Sam. He steals from Martin. Rent. Bills. Little things."

"Does Martin know?"

"Yes. Some. Martin asked Sam about money and Sam hit him in his chest. Martin coughed until blood came up."

"I don't know what I can do."

She watches me again, her thin-line mouth waiting.

The front door creaks in the next room. I stand quickly.

"You've got company."

She smoothes down her dead grass hair. "Yes," she says. "Goodbye, today."

I turn to the door.

"Hey now, what's this?" Sam rounds the corner. He's smiling. The opossum tail around his neck pulses. "Never seen you in this part of the house, Prof. I'm not dying. She's not dying."

"We were talking," Laika says.

He stares at her, his eyes making horrible promises.

"I was just leaving."

He stands blocking the door for a moment, then swings sideways. I step past. He slams his palms against my back and I fly into the opposite wall of the hallway. Laika releases a cry. I turn around and try and steady myself.

"Everything okay out there?" Martin calls from his room.

"It's all good," Sam calls back, stepping towards me, his eyes bouncing in his skull. "Just taking care of business."

Sam leans into me hard, his skin smelling of cologne.

"You better not be trying to fuck for free? You're not trying to do that are you?" His breath is in my ear. He lifts a gun and pushes the barrel against my cheek, the inside of my mouth pressing against my teeth. His cologne. It's familiar. Something in a Christmas stocking or magazine sample. "Are you? Are you trying to fuck for free?"

"Is that Drakkar or Polo?"

The handle of the gun hammers my face. Laika cries out again. A hot line of blood drips past my eye. Again, the gun hits. My body starts to fall, but Sam holds me up, turns me and pushes my face against the wall.

"Did you touch her?"

"He did not touch me."

He swings the gun at Laika. "Shut the fuck up!" Then he shoves the barrel under my chin. His other hand reaches around me and thrusts it into my pants. He grabs me in his fist. "Did you have a little touch, Doc? A sample?" He squeezes and my loins cramp. His breath on my neck, the gun pushing my chin up, he's pressed against my back and I can feel him harden. "Because that would be stealing. That would be shoplifting." He pulls his hand out and puts his palm to his nose. He sniffs. "If I ever smell her cunt on you, I will cut your dick off."

"Jesus, Sam," Martin says as he opens his door. "Leave him alone."

"This doesn't concern you," Sam says.

"Like hell, it doesn't. He's my guest."

"He was in my room."

"That's no reason to put a gun in his face."

"It's my room."

"Sam, he's leaving. He's leaving right now."

Sam looks at me. Martin nods at me. I nod.

"I'm leaving," I say. "Right now."

Sam pulls back in one fluid movement and I almost fall. He lifts his hands. "I don't want trouble with anyone." He shakes his head at me as I back to the door. "Never have."

MILES WAS ONLY FOUR MONTHS FOR HIS FIRST CHRISTMAS, TOO young to sense the season. But by his second he was a waddling, wide-eyed toddler. He marveled at our mid-sized tree glowing red and green, the lights strewn across our front yard oaks, the three stockings pinned to the frame of the front window. We bundled him up against the mild Texas cold and took him to Zilker Park so he could trot beneath the three-story tree of lights. I picked him up and spun around till he screamed with laughs.

A coffee shop on South First had a barista dress as Santa and pose with kids. He was hardly twenty, too thin and too young to play St. Nick, but he was in full costume and as enthusiastic as an amateur improv comic. Instead of the traditional red cap, this Santa bore a felt cowboy hat. He tipped it at the small gathering of children and parents. Miles found him petrifying, his body tensing and his hands squeezing the hair on the back of my head as we entered.

"It's Santa, Miles," I tried to calm him.

"Who's ready for Santa's knee?" the barista barked.

Miles's eyes, brilliantly wide and unblinking, stared in growing fear as we approached.. The barista attempted one hearty "Ho! Ho! Ho!" and Miles yelled with such terror that I jogged him out of the place, hushing him.

"No Sana. No Sana," he said. And I promised him he would never have to sit with that man or any other Santa.

With the semester over, my schedule eased. Carrie had returned to work part time, but her load that December was mild. At night, once Miles was down, Carrie and I took to sipping from a bottle of high-end scotch the dean had gifted me. We watched old movies, dozing on the living room couch in the soft light of our red and green tree and black and white films.

Something relaxed in me. In both of us. We talked about future

plans. Her returning to work full time. Finding a good daycare. We
flirted with timelines for a second child. We slept closer. I could smell
her hair, earthy and warm. I thought of telling her about the kiss—a
student's crush, a lesson learned. But our intimacy was still delicate,
our family forming. I wanted no poison in the mix.

A cold snap kept us inside and we sat on the floor with Miles
performing with stuffed animals. Carrie a giraffe, me a classic teddy,
Miles a pair of my rolled socks he'd named Bobo and come to adore.
Our avatars sat in circles, ate frozen blueberries, used the potty.

Three days before Christmas we loaded Miles into a red wagon
and walked the neighborhood, Miles clapping for each decorated
yard. "Ligh! Ligh!"

We stopped by a neighborhood party, Carrie and I filling up on
eggnog watery with whiskey. Miles chewed on star shaped cookies.
Neighbors crowded into a kitchen, patting Miles's head and laughing
surprise that it had already been a year.

"He's so big!" a woman cheered. "He'll be voting before you
know it."

I poured Carrie another cup of nog. I liked seeing her just a little
drunk, smiling loosely and laughing.

Miles fell asleep in my arms as we walked home. Carrie walked
beside us, her hand on the small of my back. She stumbled once,
tipsy and happy.

At home I laid Miles in his cot. I sat watching him sleep, watched
him reach for Bobo the rolled socks and tuck them against his cheek.
The house was quiet and glowing with Christmas lights. I was
glowing with whiskey.

I found Carrie already in bed, her eyes closed and a smile on her
face. I undressed and crawled beside her, kissing her shoulder. She
hummed sleepily and I kissed her again, slower.

"Tomorrow, I promise," she said. "It'll be your Christmas present."
She curled in to herself, her back to me. She slept.

I lay there for a bit, staring up at the pock marked ceiling. I got out
of bed and poured myself a deep drink of scotch.

I sat before the low red glow of our Christmas tree and loved and
hated my life. Would sex be an annual gift? Maybe a blowjob on my
birthday? I drank and pouted. There was my house, my tree, my
family. All the things I had gathered around me and they seemed,
at that moment, to be under the umbrella of one sad, mush word—
domestic.

Was the party still going on? Should I wander back, bring the
scotch with me? It wasn't even ten yet. The tree lights blurred with
each sip. I focused on the buzz behind the lights. A soft electric hum.
I drifted, half-sleeping.

It was much later when Miles called out.

"Dadda! Daaadda!"

I leapt from the couch, moving before I was fully awake. I found
Miles standing in his cot, his red hair scattered like a ravaged bird's
nest. He reached his arms out to me.

"Sana! Sana came to get me."

I picked him up, sloshing scotch from my half-filled glass onto his
jammies. He clung to me, his chest pulsing against mine.

"It's okay. Just a dream, Miles," I said, placing the glass on his
dresser.

He buried his head into my neck and breathed out half-cries.

I carried him into the living room, hushing him. His eyes took
in the room lit only by the soft red and green radiance of the tree.
He lay his head on my shoulder as I paced, softly singing Christmas
hymns, forgetting words and humming choruses.

His weight changed as he nodded back to sleep. He was warm, his body clutching me with unquestioning trust. He smacked his lips and exhaled his still-sweet baby breath against my neck.

My phone beeped from the coffee table. With my free hand, I picked up the phone.

A text.

An image.

Ashley, her face concealed, her body not. She lay on a green couch, her arm outstretched toward the lens, her body bare.

Miles gurgled in my ear.

Another image came through. Ashley. Again, her face out of the picture. Her body wrapped in a pink towel. The towel falling open, like theatre curtains.

I looked at her. Her body in my hand.

Another beep: "Sorry. I'm drunk."

I looked at the picture again. It burned brilliant.

She texted again: "MERRY CHRISTMAS."

I put the phone down and hummed to Miles as I carried him back to his room. I lay him in his cot, keeping a hand on his warm chest for a long minute.

When I came back to the living room, my phoned glowed with a new text. Her address.

I stared at it for a long while, then moved in a kind of stupor. I wrote a note saying I was going for milk and eggs and eased out the back door.

An insipid pop rendition of "Silent Night" played on the radio. I switched it off and drove in silence. The roads were nearly empty, the black asphalt reflecting the white lights strung from streetlight to streetlight in long arches like burning smiles.

I knew the address she'd sent. An apartment complex just north of campus. I pulled up to the curb in front of the three-story building.

Flip went the key. Quiet went the car. Red Christmas lights wrapped around the complex's tree trunks and branches illuminated my hands still on the wheel.

The engine clicked as it cooled. Through the muffle of my car I heard how this city sleeps. The near hum of the highway, the electric buzz of all these buildings, perhaps the constant flow of water through miles of pipe below me.

It was colder. I could see my breath steam in the red light.

My phone beeped. "Are you coming in?"

I leaned across to the passenger window and looked up. She stood just on the second floor balcony, her figure silhouetted against the quiet yellow of her apartment. She wore some kind of nightgown or slip—her legs a blurred V.

I wanted her. Just once. I wanted to climb those stairs and be with her only one time.

It was half past two when I got home. Standing in the driveway, I brought up the pictures of Ashley on my phone and deleted them. With a touch, she was gone.

Inside I put away the milk and eggs I'd purchased at an all-night convenience store, my head already heavy with an on-coming hangover.

Before going to bed, I paused at Miles's room. How I loved that room—its play clutter and colors, its ocean roar noisemaker, its smell of baby. Through the door I could see his small form, quiet in his cot. He was growing so long. Soon he'd move to a bed. Soon he'd be a little boy. The mobile drifted above him.

I did not make love to Ashley Briggers. I never even left the car. Why?

To honor my wife, our marriage, the trust between us? Yes. But the rawest reason, the motivation base enough to battle the lust of a thirty-something with a willing and beautiful twenty-something, was fear. I did not make love to her because I believed bad things would happen if I did. I believed in some mystic mathematical equation that my wrongdoing, my breaking of a wedding vow, would garner some kind of punishment.

I thought the world worked that way.

Soon it would be Christmas morning. Soon Miles would be waking up and I'd lift him from his cot. He'd totter into the living room holding my hand and he'd find a stocking and presents and Carrie waiting. We would watch him tear into the stocking, watch him unwrap the handmade wooden rolling rabbit Carrie had bought at a farmers market. We'd eat pancakes and sip coffee and be a family. I had not slept with Ashley Briggers. I had passed some kind of test.

I turned from Miles's door and I headed to bed. I'd later learn that at that moment he was almost certainly already dead.

THEY TOOK MILES'S BODY ON CHRISTMAS MORNING. THEY TOOK photos of the cot—but there was nothing there. Nothing deadly. Nothing but his cot. Wasn't it the safest spot in our house?

We were told he was taken to the medical examiner's office. We were told there would be an autopsy to determine the cause of death. We were told so many things. It all came through like whistles in a windstorm.

They asked what happened. We asked the same. What had happened?

"Did you hear anything in the night?" they asked. "A cough or a cry?"

"Nothing. Nothing." Carrie said.

"He woke once," I said. "He cried and I sang him back down."

"And what time was that?"

"I don't know . . ."

"Your best guess, sir."

"Eleven. Maybe midnight."

And they scribbled everything down.

We were given a death certificate. Cause of death read *undetermined.*

A rattling word. A useless word.

Those next days were the dark twin of Miles's first days of life.

His death—his absence—was like waking to a world with no sky. Or an earth with no ground. Disorienting in every way. We found every detail confusing. I stumbled on floor stains. She gagged on her toothbrush.

People swamped us with casseroles and condolences. And my body, to my distaste, functioned. I was hungry, so I ate. I was sleepy, so I slept. My body was still alive.

We reached for a sponge and the cabinet door caught, our home still child safe. We opened the fridge and his yogurt cups lay in wait. We woke in the night to phantom cries, jumping from bed and tripping into the hall before remembering there's no child to comfort.

Panic leapt out from any corner of the house. A light switch, a creaking step, the dropping mail would send us sweating and shaking and unable to name a reason. Something had to be done, now, right now! But there was nothing to do.

Jesus, oh, Jesus, I believed—as I had been taught by every film, every song, every Easter sermon—that love could conquer all. That love could survive all. It is not true.

The funeral was New Year's Day. A cold, bright day.

People stared in awe at us. Carrie and I were an ocean of grief— incomprehensibly deep and long. They could not take it in.

The child's coffin. Varnished. I think we chose it. Smell of furniture polish and the sick sweet of air freshener. The minister at St. Christopher's read some things, said some things, sentiment that fell into the ocean like rice. We stood by a display of photos and toys. We hugged and shook hands and somehow did everything we were supposed to do as if we'd been instructed.

People approached, curious and mouth-sick. Some touched us. Some hugged. How do you hug the ocean? Some threw lies and promises believing they could fill us up. Believing that if enough "he's in a better place" and "God has called him home" piled up on the bottom, then the hollow would be at least partially filled. But as soon as the words left their mouth and disappeared into our eyes, even as we nodded our gratitude, they could see how dead their condolences were. They stepped away.

Others chose, even there in the church's lunch hall, to share their own disasters. Lost loved ones, early deaths. I wanted to say to each of them, stop, please don't say any more. Please don't believe, as surely you didn't believe, that this grief is one of a billion, that this death is one of a billion billion billion. Please. There is no comfort there.

At home, after the funeral, Carrie undressed and got into bed, though it was only five in the evening.

I paced the house. My study, books and books.. I touched the spines, cool and present. I knew every word on every page was dead. Through the floorboards above me I could hear her cry in her sleep.

At sunfall I watched the light retreat from our backyard. The same yard, same trees and sky. The spirit had evacuated. The world still had all the parts, but the soft hum had gone. The world is a corpse.

There's a thin veil between our days and reality. It's woven from habits, meals, duties, chores, television shows, soccer practices, traffic jams, Christmas, coffee breaks, sex, and debt. Occasionally the veil rips and the cold sandy truth of it all blows through the tear. We race to mend it with a drink or a new hobby or a book. Then slowly reinforce the stitching with thoughtlessness and forgetfulness.

A big enough rip and you get more than just a gush of reality, you get a view. And it's nothing. Desert dead. Less. Wind with sand. And love did not make me strong. My love for Miles has left me as exposed as a lidless eye.

The police called the following morning.

My wife's sister had come by early with a bag of bagels and was trying to get us to eat. She chattered away, flitting about the house like a trapped bird. When the call came from the police station requesting I come down and sign some mandatory papers, I was glad for an excuse to leave.

I drove to the police station by the courthouse where I had once paid a parking fine. A polite officer led me from the lobby through swinging doors and down a hallway. He opened a door to a beige-walled room with a table and three chairs and a two-way mirror. He told me to wait there and someone would soon be with me.

Then he left and I sat down, my stomach turning. I knew they were watching. What were they watching for? What did they think I'd done?

After ten minutes two men in dark suits came in and sat across the table from me. The taller, older one stared down his long, drooping face. The other man, young with thin, animated eyebrows, smiled as he straightened a manila file tapping the pages into place.

"So," said the younger one. "Want to tell us what happened?"

"I don't understand what's going on," I said.

He smiled apologetically, his eyebrows arching. "I'm sorry." He cleared his throat. "We're trying to find out what exactly happened to your son."

The other kept staring, his jowls sagging, looking like he might doze off at any moment. The younger one cleared his throat again. "Wouldn't you like to tell us what really happened that night?"

"What do you think happened?" I asked.

"We really don't know." He smiled, nearly chuckled. "But we'd like to find out."

"One thing is certain," the older one said. "Your son did not die of natural causes."

The muscles in my neck clenched. I blinked and shook my head.

"Mr. Bonds," said the younger one, looking down into the file. "Can you tell us why your son was doused with alcohol?"

"With what?"

"Had you been drinking that night?" he asked. "Christmas Eve. You'd been drinking, right?"

"I had a drink or two."

"Mr. Bonds," the older one said. "You took out a fifty thousand dollar life insurance policy on your son."

"Excuse me?"

"You've made a hefty profit from all this."

"The insurance?" I asked. It all made no sense. "It was a package deal the university offered. I . . ."

"Of course, of course," said the younger one. "We just want all the facts out there."

I looked from one to the other—dancing eyebrows to drooping jowls.

"Shouldn't I have a lawyer?"

The younger one's eyebrows stretched high. "Of course, if you'd like. Or we could just talk it out. Work it out right here."

"I think I'd like to have my lawyer here."

The younger one looked at me as if I hadn't said anything. As if I'd come to my senses and talk. I did nothing. Finally he looked to his partner who gave the slightest shrug. The younger one opened his folder and made a mark inside of it.

Without another word they left me alone.

I sat alone, cold panic pumping through me, a strange icy terror. I paced the room. Why was I there? I should have been with Carrie. I needed to call her. I needed to go home. I stepped toward the door just as it reopened and the two men reentered. The older man asked

me to turn around and placed handcuffs on my wrists as the younger
one explained I was being arrested on suspicion of the murder of
Miles Bonds.

The world went muffled and unreal. They led me down the hall
into a bright, florescent space where officers took my wallet, my
phone, my keys. They pressed my fingers to ink. They photographed
me. There was waiting and papers and hallways. I found my body
doing whatever they asked. Standing, walking, turning to the left,
urinating. I would have done anything they said.

Within an hour my lawyer, Tom Hobart, had arrived and we were
left to talk in a different beige-walled jailhouse meeting room. This
one had no mirror.

"They think you killed your boy," he said. "They're going for negligent homicide."

Tom had been our lawyer since a car accident Carrie had been
in six years before, a not-so-serious hit-and-run by a drunk driver.
He was a ruddy, robust man, fifteen years my elder, with constantly red and irritated skin as if he'd just shaved with an overused razor.

"I don't understand," I said. "I didn't do anything."

"They'll formerly charge you today. I'll aim for a reasonable bail
so we can get you out of here."

"But what did I do wrong?"

"Felony cases go to a grand jury first. They determine whether
there's enough question to go to trial. This won't move fast."

"They said he didn't die of natural causes."

"The autopsy was inconclusive, that's all. Inconclusive," he said.
"It's standard that they investigate the closest relatives."

"I didn't do anything."

"My God, Oliver, stop saying that. I know." Tom rubbed his

cheeks with one hand. "But the autopsy was inconclusive and, well, god damn it, little boys don't just up and die."

"Why do they think . . ."

"A parent is always the first suspect in these cases. Nine times out of ten it's one of the parents."

"I didn't hurt my son,"

"I know, I know." Tom reached out and patted my hand. His hand felt warm, almost feverish. "We've got a long way to go. A lot of little bureaucratic steps." He sighed as if he were already weary of the process. "How's Carrie holding up?"

I shook my head.

They charged me—a judge, young and well-groomed, sitting behind cheap wood panels—charged me with negligent homicide. It happened quickly. No fanfare, no thunder. Just a poker-faced judge telling me the state aimed to prove I killed my son.

After the proceedings, before they took me back into my cell, Tom turned to me, puffing out his cheeks and exhaling.

"This happens," he said. "Happens to good people. To good parents, just like you. Could happen to anybody. My kids are all grown now, but, oh, there but for the grace of God go I."

I sat in my cell and I thought about that phrase—*there but for the grace of God go I*. I had used the phrase. Carrie, I remembered, had said the same thing when our neighbor had wrestled his son from out of our living room. I know its intent. Tom was trying to comfort me. But the phrase's meaning is wretched: "Oliver, I'm just like you. Except I have God's grace upon me and so do my children."

Or more concisely: "If God didn't love me, I'd be you."

An hour later, I walked out of jail. Carrie paid my bail, thousands more than I thought we had. She drove me home speaking constantly.

How dare they. Goddamn them. Outrageous.

She was furious and energized. That vast expanse of pain was directed like a river into this injustice.

"I talked to Tom," she said as she parked the car in the drive. "He's optimistic. It's just a political stunt, that's all."

I wanted to be angry, as indignant as Carrie, but I was shelled out. The week had carved me empty and the day had boiled me out with doubt. What *had* I done? I had done something. Babies don't just die. Things happen for a reason. Things happen.

We walked toward the house and a new quiet fell. We stepped inside. It was silent, empty. A universe of empty. A flower arrangement from the funeral sat on the dining room table smelling foully sweet.

I started to cry and she reached out and took my hand.

She made me a sandwich and left me at the kitchen table.

She called her mother and then her sister, telling them all we knew, repeating the phrase, "He's optimistic. It's just a political stunt, that's all."

I sat wordless. Restless and tight, these new doubts shrinking my skin. I went to bed and lay sleepless.

I could hear her below—another call, same words. I could hear her anger running out, her steps slowing, like an engine on an empty tank.

Finally she came to bed. She crawled in next to me and we listed to the house. I wanted to sleep for years and wake up not feeling all of this. But the sleep was cracked—dreams and half dreams. Both of us fitful and sick.

At some hour we crawled into each other half-asleep like two drowning men. Her body hot and mine shaking, making silent, grasping love. Not a word or sound until I came inside her and she screamed. A terrified scream.

I rolled away—bile in my throat. I understood. Oh God, I understood what made her scream. To conceive that night would be a horror. It would produce a ghost child, an unwanted echo of Miles.

But as we lay there in the dark, both stricken, both alien to the other, even at that moment a baby was beginning inside her body.

OLAF AND HIS FATHER SAILED FURTHER NORTH, AWAY FROM THE BAR-
ricade of ice. The weather grew warmer with each day, becoming
nearly tropic. Massive colorful birds, unrecognized by either, flew
overhead, calling out to one another in high squeals and whistles. A
pod of narwhals lumbered past, graceful and large.

"We've reached Avalon, Father!"

Their compass jumped from limp to frantic, then pushed upward
against the glass and refused to move. After ten days, it corrected
itself and pointed straight north. But Olaf's father was sure that they
had passed the northern tip days before. Surely they were now sailing
south.

They came to one patch of land, their first in a month—a dot of
jungle rimmed by white sand. Here they anchored, restocked their
supplies, and slept on solid earth for the first time in months.

In the dull pre-dawn light, they sailed on. As they skirted the
shore of the island, a solitary boy, naked and tall, stepped from the
foliage, his skin as translucent as wet paper, nearly glowing in the
soft morning light. Olaf called to him, waving his arms. The boy
watched, not moving or returning the calls but for a slow smile. His
teeth were black, as black as unfinished ebony and sharpened to
points. Black small teeth in a red, wet mouth.

MAP of the Interior World.

BEYOND
THE ICE

"We have come into our own," my father said to me. "This is the fulfillment of the tradition told me by my father and my father's father, and still back for many generations of our race. This is, assuredly, the land beyond the North Wind." —Olaf Jansen

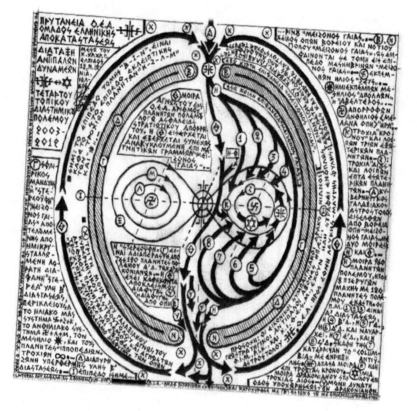

As I'm walking down the gravel drive from the shed, Jenny steps from salon and calls out to me.

"Yo, Ollie. You got a call this morning. A guy named Martin. He nearly coughed a lung through the phone line."

I take a deep breath and step toward her door.

"Friend of yours?" she asks.

"Dear friend," I say.

Using the salon's counter phone, I call. Martin sounds groggy and slow.

"Were you sleeping?" I ask.

"Been up since five." He coughs. "Having trouble getting moving today."

"You need anything?"

"Chemo. Metro says I didn't reserve a ride. I know I did. I always do." He coughs again. "I don't mind. I hate that shit."

"Martin. You can't skip these."

"I'm actually feeling pretty good." He coughs so loud I have to hold the phone from my ear. Jenny cringes.

"Is Sam . . ."

"He's not here. Just me."

"What time is your appointment, Martin?"

I get the information, hang up and call Lyle.

"Dude," he says. "Get your ass to REI."

"The camping store?"

"Get on a bus and get here now!"

Tents hover in a suspended rapture and the vast room smells of nylon and trail mix. I hear Lyle almost immediately.

"Oh no, I want the neon one. Something you'll see in the snow."

I find him near the back towering over a young woman in hiking shorts and a worn smile.

"Does this glow in the dark?"

"No, sir."

"It should. That would be awesome."

"It would make it hard to sleep with a glowing coat in your tent."

"Oh shit, that is so true—Ollie!" He slaps my back. "This is Janet. She's helping us stock up. Janet, I'm going to need a matching coat—Teflon, is that right?—a matching one but a few sizes down."

Lyle is decked out in a bright green neon jacket, a felt camping fedora, and yellow polarized glasses. He hands me the glasses off of his face.

"Try these. They actually make things brighter. It's amazing."

"Lyle, these glasses cost four hundred bucks. How are you going to pay for these?"

He whips out a Visa credit card. "I'm not."

"You know how those work, right? You do pay, eventually."

"Not if I don't come back." He turns to a full-length mirror and admires himself. "I woke up this morning thinking, Jesus, I'm so worried about money. Why? We're either staying down there—and you know they don't have money —or we *do* come back, we'll have proof, we'll be getting money thrown at us. Either way, my days of material worries are coming to an end. And there it was in the mail. Visa begging me to spend their money."

"It's not their money you're spending."

"I made the call and got the card. It was more than easy. They said they could only advance me five thousand as cash. I've got these credit checks. I figure we send one to Horner, or give it to him in person at the book signing. It doesn't quite cover even the down payment, but it shows we're trying." He turns back to the mirror. "He's got to respect that, right?"

"Sir," Janet says, handing me a neon coat. "Are you going to need the thermal underwear and . . ."

"He needs it all. We're going into the ice, Janet! Fortress of Solitude ice."

"Lyle, I need to ask a favor," I say as Janet walks off, frowning. "My friend Martin needs a ride to chemotherapy today."

"Shit," Lyle says, lowering the headlamp he'd been admiring. "Kind of freaky."

"I'll owe you, Lyle."

"You already do."

I let Martin take the front seat and I squeeze into the back of Lyle's car. Lyle has given in to the warmth and removed his neon green coat, but the polarized glasses never leave his face.

"Hey Ollie," Martin says. "Sorry again for Sam the other day. That was uncalled for."

"It's not your fault."

"I had a long talk with him. Told him how it is. How a house has rules. So it won't happen again. I can promise that," he says. "I don't want you to feel you can't come by. I'd hate that."

"I'll keep coming."

"Good, good." He nods. "Sam helps me out more than you know. Other day I was walking, I was just walking out to the Caddy. And my legs went jelly. Sam picked me up like a baby. Scary as shit. Just picked me up like I was a little baby and there was nothing I could do. If Sam hadn't been there, I'd have spent all night on the driveway."

"You've got a Cadillac?" Lyle asks.

"A sweet '88. Work on it everyday," Martin says, grinning. "By the time I get it running I won't be able to drive it."

Both he and Lyle smoke. I can feel my teeth yellow with every breath.

It doesn't take long to get there and Martin leads us to oncology.

The hospital waiting room is white and beige. The plants are green and healthy. The floor is clean and shining. The art is pastel and calm. Only the patients are ragged.

Martin struts in and the nurse behind the counter smiles. "Mr. Dale," she says. "You made it. Now that's more like it." She's in her fifties and has a southern twang, smiling like a politician's wife. "Now take a seat and we'll get you back there fast."

"The nurses love me," Martin says. "Always flirting. I hate doctors. But nurses are all right."

We wait for nearly an hour before the nurse calls Martin and he struts back into the treatment rooms. Lyle stands, too.

"Let's check out the gift store."

It feels good to leave that waiting room. Even a hospital hallway is more cheerful.

The gift store is a small, cluttered affair. Happy new baby dolls and balloons, rows of condolence and get well cards, boxes of candy and chocolates fill the room. Lyle digs through a bucket of discounted beanbag animals.

Miles was born here.

You'd think the *It's a Boy!* balloons and cards would get me. You'd think maybe I'd break down. But it's never when I expect it. I don't weep when *Cats in the Cradle* plays on the radio or a public service billboard shows a father with his son on his lap. My guard is up and I can clearly see the threat. It's the surprises that get me. Fingernail clippings and the smell of applesauce.

"Your friend," Lyle says, reading the label on a beanbag turkey. "Does he have any money?"

"Does he look like he has any money?"

"He's got a Cadillac." Lyle picks out a beanbag turkey. "Maybe ask him."

The sky has turned gray by the time we leave. Martin is gray, too.

"How'd it go," I ask as we walk to the car, his steps slow and unsure.

"They hook me up and give me the shit and tell me to leave."

"How do you feel?" I ask.

"I feel like I've freebased a can of bug killer."

"Here, Marty." Lyle hands him the beanbag turkey as we reach the car. "A little pick-me-upper. If you hold on to it, it can catch a sweet price on eBay."

Martin nods.

Driving down I-35, a few dirty raindrops hit the windshield.

"I don't have wipers, so we're just going to let this one ride," Lyle says as he lights a cigarette. I'm in the back again.

"Thanks for the turkey, Lyle. I got a nephew who's gonna love it."

"My pleasure, Marty," Lyle says. "Want a smoke?"

"Not just yet."

"Cancer is a real bitch, huh Marty?" Lyle says.

"Never truer words."

"Don't let this cancer call the shots. You know?" Lyle says. There's a shift in his tone I don't like.

"Sure. I'm going to beat it."

"I'm saying, you call the shots, not the cancer. Get me?" Lyle says, pulling in smoke. "Check out on your own accord."

"Lyle," I say.

"I'm in no rush to die," Martin says.

"I hear that, brother. I hear that," Lyle says. "But the time is coming and you're either going to walk out of the building or get carried out in a box."

"Lyle, I say. "I want you to shut up."

"It's okay," Martin says. "Ain't as if the thought hasn't crossed my mind. But I'm doing fine. I can still beat this."

"No one beats death," Lyle says.

"Jesus did."

"Maybe," Lyle says. "He had to die first. I call that a tie."

"Lyle, you need to shut up right now," I say.

"Hey, my car," he says. "Show some respect." He offers the open cigarette package to Martin. "I say make it your call. Get a friend to help. Tell cancer to fuck itself." Lyle nods at me. I stare back at him, my anger moving in my stomach like a crab.

"I hear what you're saying, Lyle," Martin says, taking a cigarette. "But I don't want to die yet."

"No rush," Lyle says, handing over his lighter. "See how you feel in a month."

We say nothing for the rest of the drive. Lyle flips through radio channels, hopping between a libertarian pundit and hip-hop.

He pulls to the curb in front of Martin's. I climb out and face Lyle.

"You stay here," I say.

He raises his palms. "Fine. But make it quick." Then leans back in his seat.

I help Martin from the car and up the drive to his door. He's like a worn out luggage bag, shoulder bones sticking out like wire hangers, skin loose and thin. He fumbles with his keys at the door, finally managing it open.

He makes it through the house on his own and I help him lower into his recliner. "I am tired," he says. "Just wiped out tired."

"I'm sorry about Lyle," I say.

"Don't be. Like I said, I've thought about it."

I don't say anything.

"Truth is, Ollie, sometimes I feel like the delivery man's standing at the door, but he won't hand the damn package over."

"I can understand that," I say.

His closes his eyes, leaning his head back. "I don't think the cancer is going to kill me."

"You don't huh?"

"I'm not going to die in some god-forsaken hospital room. No, if

I have to die, I'll die on the road," he says, smiling with eyes closed. "Going west. West is always beautiful."

"Yeah."

"On the road in my Cadillac, windows open. That's how I'd like to go," he says in almost a whisper.

"It'd be hell for your passengers."

He gives a raspy chuckle. "Maybe I'll let you take the wheel."

"I don't drive."

"Still up for lunch this week?"

"Always," I say.

Lyle is waiting, I know. But I stay until Martin falls asleep.

I find Laika on the step in front of Martin's house, facing the black street and piles of unpicked up trash, a wet couch rotting in the hot sun. Lyle sits in his car, his head back. I presume his eyes are closed, though the polarized glasses make it hard to say.

She's smoking, her left eye bruised purple and yellow.

"You stayed away," she says.

"I was told to."

"You chose to."

"What did he do?" I ask.

"He left me."

I pause, confused. "Sam?"

"My husband," she says. "He wrote. He divorced me."

I sit on the cement facing her, bending my legs like a pretzel.

"He waited, too," she says. "The date on the paper. The date is last month. But he waits until I send another check. One last check from my great, wonderful computer job. And then he sends the divorce. They will not come here. Not him, not my daughter."

"He's a prick."

"I've had worse." She drags her cigarette and squints her bruised eye at the sun. "I have no plan now. Just do what I'm doing. And I owe Sam money and he won't . . ."

She trails off. I look at her. I look at her eyes. Her bruised face. I look for a long time without looking away. She turns to me and I still don't look away. She seems to study my gaze, trying to interpret it. Then she frowns and flicks her cigarette away.

"Your son died, yes."

"Yes," I say.

"That is very horrible," she says.

Her face softens, just for moment,. But she won't allow it. She looks out to the street and closes her eyes. Then she stands, her waist even with my face. I can see the silhouette of her legs through the thin fabric of her dress.

She looks down at me, the sun behind her. She touches my head.

I want this.

I want to bury my face in her dress. I want to raise her dress and pull her crotch to me.

"There is nothing I do not hate about my life," she says.

I look up. She's studying something far away.

"In half an hour another customer comes. I know him. He has come before. And he does not smell good and his skin feels wrong. And he mumbles the whole time. Mumbles in my face. And I will hold my breath. And I cannot even say I am doing this for my daughter or my husband. I have no reason."

"Then—"

"I will do it. This I already know. I will do it. But I have no reason."

"You're a self-centered dickhead," I say as we drive down North Lamar away from Martin's neighborhood.

"Self-centered?" Lyle is genuinely shocked. "I just spent a whole day driving your sick-ass friend around town."

"You also suggested he take his own life. Or more specifically, that I take his life."

"I'd help," he says, running a stale yellow. "The guy is rotting. Sometimes it's just time to check out. You can ruin a good party by staying past your welcome."

"Oh my God, Lyle, staying past your welcome is what you're best at."

"Now you're just being mean," he says, swerving through lanes. "This is a gift. I was offering a gift."

"For a price."

"Look, Marty has a need, a way out of a shitty death sentence. We need twenty thousand dollars this week and my guess is he has some money he can't spend. I'm trying to think outside the box."

"Jesus, Lyle. His name isn't Marty. It's Martin." I punch the dash. "Do you ever, ever, ever think about other people."

Lyle yanks the car into a Stop & Shop parking lot and slams to a halt. The seatbelt strains against my body. He turns his bulk to me.

"Fuck you, Ollie. Fuck you," he says, poking a finger into my chest. "I've been busting my ass being your friend. Trying to save your fucking life. I'm trying everything I know to get you to do something. To do anything. Get you laid or get you out of town and all I get from you is whining and crying. I mean, Marty's more alive than you and he's half-dead. You're afraid of everything." He faces forward, breathing hard. "I need some cigarettes."

He kills the engine, climbs from the car, and slams the door.

And here I am, alone in the car. The air is still and hot, singed with flat cigarette smoke and carbon monoxide. The plastic and metal expands, clicks and pops in the new quiet. Minutes pass and the air tightens. Another car pulls away, muffled and distant. I see Lyle inside sorting through the top of the magazine rack.

I know why I hate him. It's not because he's wrong. He's asking the right question. Why don't I die? Everything has been taken, but this last bit I can still snatch. Why not steal that privilege from the universe? To not be. To not feel this or be this.

Sun through the windshield and hot unmoving air. Sweat beads on my forehead. The sea belt strap holds me to the hot plastic. Sweat rolls into my eyes. I blink, I blink and my eyes burn. I will not remove my seat belt. I will not open my door. I blink, mouth and head watering. Blink.

I open the door and the car inhales. I'm breathing, my eyes wet with sweat, and my relief proves Lyle to be a truthsayer. I am afraid of everything.

I unclick my seatbelt and climb from the car. Lyle walks from the store saying something, but I'm too far gone.

After the arrest came the press with cameras and questions. Carrie and I locked the door, closed the curtains, and silenced the phone. We barricaded ourselves in.

We tried to live. But Carrie and I could hardly move in our home without a reminder. Our house was infested with memories. Unused diapers, the crib cushions, the plastic giraffe Miles refused to release from his tiny grip for months, the breast milk frozen in the freezer—yellow and stone—the stereo flipped on three weeks after and playing music box Mozart. Every corner held artifacts of Miles's life, or our life as parents that filled our house. Our house was haunted.

We drove to see his grave, the only time since his burial. The stone and the grass—the place had no connection to my son. I hope to never see that place again.

While Carrie and I were away, her sister, with sinister kindness, cleaned. She scrubbed and gathered and removed all trace of Miles's life with us. We arrived home as she was finishing. She had left pictures on the wall - decorations. But the detritus—pacifiers, plastic spoons, and mobiles—were gone. The house smelled of air freshener and bleach. She had scrubbed the smell of my son from my home and there she stood in our living room with a half-smile asking not to be thanked, proud and teary. I hated her. I told her I hated her.

"Ollie," Carrie said, shaking her head.

"How did we let them wash his body?" I said to Carrie. "They didn't even know him, Carrie. How did we let them have his body? We should have dressed him. We should have put him in jammies and sang to him, Carrie. We should have hummed to him when they closed it up. His smell, Carrie. His smell should still be with us."

For a time we had grieved together, crying into each other, protecting the other's silence. Without words we agreed to not talk about Miles or the case or anything, like two burn victims agreeing not to touch.

Carrie and I had a healthy, good love. Solid, that's how you would have described us. "Oh, Oliver and Carrie. They've got a solid marriage. Solid as a rock."

For a time the other was comforter and protector. But the air in our home soured.

She boiled water though she didn't want tea. I picked up the remote and put it back down again without clicking a button. She said she was going to take a shower, but did not. I lay out on the couch and closed my eyes, but did not sleep.

It was worse than being alone. The other was an audience. And now it was clear the other had always been only an audience, that for the last seven years we had paced on separate, opposing stages simultaneously performing and reacting to the other's performance. Then came the wonderful outcome of our performance. The baby.

We paused and watched. And without discussion we both directed our own performances toward him. His laugh was the finest sound this earth has ever made. His first laugh was inspired by one of Carrie's new nursing bras fresh from the laundry and dangling over his head. He chuckled, high-pitched and full of gurgles.

"Evolution worked for a billion years just to produce that sound," I said to Carrie. "Once you hear that, you'll do anything to protect him."

All this time, as we mourned and clung and waited as affidavits were filed, there was a secret growing in my wife. When she first told me, I didn't hear.

"Pregnant," she said again, trying to smile. "The doctor said I'm pregnant."

I stayed very still. We were in our kitchen, me sitting, she standing, her hands behind her gripping the countertop.

"Well?" she asked.

"I don't see how that is possible." Which was a lie. I remembered the scream. It was the one time we'd made love since his death. Even without that I knew the impossible was all very possible.

"I'm four weeks in."

"What do you want to do?"

"What do you mean?"

"I mean, what do you want to do?"

"I don't want to do anything."

The refrigerator hummed and every surface still glowed bleach from my sister-in-law's housekeeping.

"It's not right," I said.

"What's not right?"

"It's not fair to Miles."

"Not fair to Miles?" She released the countertop and crossed her arms in front of her chest. "There's a baby growing in me Ollie, a little baby. I mean, it's kind of a miracle. It *is* a miracle."

I shook my head. "Miles . . ."

"This isn't Miles, Ollie."

We couldn't say a thing.

Her body changed as the weeks progressed. A slight bulge, morning nausea, and she smiled. She grinned. With all her energy, she urged her grief to transmute into something new.

I could not touch her. Whatever it was growing in her was alien and unreal. Miles's usurper.

And something as heavy, as demanding, was growing in me. Carrie saw hers as an answer. Mine was a question.

So we shared our house, both growing a sickness inside.

She slept nights. I walked the house, finally dozing for an hour or two in my study. I'd wake just before dawn and climb the stairs to our room. She'd be rising, preparing to leave for Big Stacy Pool or pre-natal yoga. The day was hers, the night mine. We shared only those gray, voiceless moments in between.

We both still cried, but never in the same room.

The legal wheels were turning. But the whole thing moved slow and unreal. Requests for dismissals. Rescheduling. Submissions and papers and nothing concrete.

I retreated to the university, pointlessly filling an office. She had lunches. She started back at work. We sank into ourselves like butterflies reverting to pupa. She closed her wings about her body and disappeared from me, and me from her. We remerged changed and alien to one another.

She was a mother. I was something else.

One afternoon I came home and heard her laughing. That sound in our house was gross, absurd. And another voice was with her.

I found her and Manuel Cruz in Miles's room. The floor was draped with a white drop cloth. Manuel held a dripping roller. Carrie stood in overalls, a smudge on her cheek like she was a Home Depot ad.

"Hey Oliver," Manuel said, subduing his laughter.

"What are you doing?" I asked.

Carrie smiled—that new untrue smile. That *trying* smile that I despised.

"It's called Sunrise Yellow. They say it mellows when it dries. I hope to God it does."

The room was grotesque and changed.

"What are you doing?" I said again.

"I know it's a little early. But I figured we'd get a jump on things." She kept the smile there, but it was dying in the corners, rotting on her face like bad fruit.

"Now, Oliver," Manuel said, his voice bloated with compassion. "I know you're hurting. But—"

I walked from the room. Carrie followed, grabbing my shoulder in the hallway. Whispering angry.

"Oliver, this doesn't mean I love Miles any less."

"Of course it does. Of course it does."

I watch the water boil, the dry noodles in my hand. The water steams to nothing. I refill the pot from my shower and begin again. On the third pot, I drop the Ramen in. The bubbles pause when the noodles hit, the heat trying to catch up.

From outside, a squeak on the steps. I pause.

A knock on the door.

Lyle wouldn't knock. Miller would yell. No one else would visit.

"Oliver? Can I come in?"

Ashley inches the door open, holding a pumpkin in her arms and dangling a bottle of wine from between her fingers. "Is this an okay time?"

"You startled me."

"I'm terrifying." She hands me the pumpkin. "Corkscrew?"

"Sorry, no." I place the pumpkin down on the table beside the boiling noodles. She looks flushed and beautiful.

"Hope it's all right I hunted you down." she says, opening my one kitchen-area drawer and rummaging for a corkscrew.

"How did you find me?"

"John Hendon. He pointed the way."

In November the weather dropped to below freezing for a few nights, and I invited John Hendon and two others Agape regulars to share my shack. Mr. Miller was not pleased.

"Wait, it's screw top. We're saved!" She grabs two coffee cups and begins pouring from the bottle.

She puts the cup in my hand. She's been drinking. That's clear. She clinks her mug to mine and takes a long swallow. I don't.

Now her eyes study the space and she hums a little. She picks up a fork and stirs the noodles. "Salt keeps the noodles from sticking, have any?"

"No."

"Well, I never minded sticky noodles." She looks at me, her eyes suddenly younger. "Is it okay that I'm here?"

I place the cup down. "You brought a pumpkin."

"Yes!" she turns from the pot. "I saw it at the store and I thought, hell, pumpkins are hollow." She knocks her knuckles against it. "Why not earth?"

She grabs a knife from the drawer and stabs the pumpkin, cutting with quick jerks. "I say if it happens in the small it can happen in the large. Right? So check it out." She lifts a lid from the pumpkin and motions for me to look. I stare in.

"So the world is a pumpkin," she says.

"It rings like a bell," I say.

"What?"

"When a planet is hit by an asteroid or anything, the planet rings like a bell. The one that killed the dinosaurs must have echoed for decades."

"And there's holes, you said? Ways in."

"Many. Some small and undiscovered. The biggest are at the poles." I turn the burner off and the boiling ends. "Why are you here, Ashley?"

"I like talking to you," she says. She stares for a long moment. "You never wrote me. Not a word. Not a phone call."

"What would I have said?"

"Everyone thought I was lying. The police, my lawyer, my dad. Everyone thought I knew more than I was saying." She sits on the cot. "My dad thought I was going to jail. I thought I was, too."

"For what?"

"For helping to murder your son."

"I didn't—"

"I know." She holds her mug in both hands. "Doesn't matter much."

"Whether I killed my son?"

"I was the one who found my mom," she says into the mug. "I was going out for the night and she didn't want me to leave. We argued. I was supposed to be home at midnight, but I stayed out till two, came home and found her on the floor."

"She didn't kill herself because you went out."

"The coroner said she took a bottle of pills at 11:45." She looked at me with desperate eyes, desperate for me to understand. "She was waiting for me. She thought I'd come home and find her alive, and I'd call an ambulance. She didn't plan on dying. But I didn't come home on time. She was waiting, and I didn't come."

"I'm sorry," I say.

She shakes her head. "I feel like I killed her. I know that's crazy, but I feel it. And then they tell me I helped kill your little boy."

"You didn't."

"I know I didn't. Jesus." She stops. "But I did make you leave your house." She looks back into her mug. "I did try . . ."

There's a long quiet and I watch her sitting there. She's still so young. I had never once, not even once, thought about how everything had hit her. Miles was mine and Carrie's. It was our tragedy, but, of course, it was hers, too.

"Ashley," I say. "It's not your fault."

She looks up at me, nodding, her eyes wet and dark. "You could have told me that."

She wipes her eyes and exhales a long breath.

"So, this is funny," she says. "In grad school I hooked up with this professor. Kind of looked like you." She glances at me. "I think I had to get it out of my system, you know?" She stands, picks up the bottle and pours more wine. "I broke his heart. Never knew I had it in me. I mean, I was always the shy one. I could never even speak to you. But Roger, that was his name, Roger called me ten times a day for a month begging me to . . . well, I don't even know what he wanted. Finally I threatened to tell his wife and I never heard from him again."

"He was married?"

"With kids." She smiles—it's a mix of shame and pride. "Can you imagine? Really, I never knew I was the type. And you know what?"

"Tell me."

"I was *cruel* to him."

She looks at me for a long time. Maybe she's waiting for me to forgive her this as well? Maybe I'm her confessor? Or maybe it's a proposition and she's waiting for my answer.

"It's hollow. It's not empty."

"What?" she says.

"The pumpkin," I say. "And the earth. It's hollow. But it's not empty. I want to know what's in there."

She moves to the pumpkin and looks in. I join her, our heads close, staring into the mass of orange webbing and seeds.

"What do you see?" I ask.

"It's like spider webs," she says. "Or maybe a nervous system."

"I see angels," I say. "Yellow and orange wings."

I watch her. Her skin is yogurt and rose. She raises her head and sees me looking. She leans across the pumpkin and kisses my neck just below the jawbone. I don't move.

"I'm not a professor anymore," I say.

"I'm not a student."

She steps to me and lifts her hands to my face. She leaves them there until the heat comes through. How long? How long since I was touched?

"If I kiss you," she says. "Will you kiss me back?"

She moves close to me and her body brushes back and forth across mine, and though I'm wordless through and through, she hushes me. And I know I will kiss her. I will lose all I can in her.

She draws closer. "Poor thing," she breathes. "Poor thing."

I think back to my office, and a younger Ashley, and that injured grackle she cradled in. She has the same look now as she did then. That same thrilled pity. Only now it's a shed, not a university office. Only now it's me, not a dying bird. I'm flapping useless wings and it thrills her.

I step back. Her eyes narrow, considering me..

"I think I should have some more wine," she says, picking up the bottle.

In an hour's time the wine bottle is empty and Ashley lies stretched out on my bed.

"It's so bright," she says with a yawn.

I switch off the lamp and sit on my chair. Squirrels chase and dance above us. I hear her breathing.

"I don't want to steal your bed," she says. "Do you want to lay down with me?"

For some reason I can smell her better in the dark. The cool smell of cut flowers and her red wine breath. I don't move from my chair. I listen to her breathing. She must be asleep. But then she speaks.

"What do you think you'll find in there? Angels?"

"Answers," I say.

"Do you want to know a secret?" she says, her voice sleepy and a little drunk. "Life is not fair and the universe doesn't care."

"Maybe," I say. "But we want it to be fair, don't we. Don't we all think it *should* be fair? I mean, is it possible that compassion is just something we made up?"

"Sure," she says.

"And the universe has no justice, no real kindness, no soul."

"Maybe we're the soul," she says. "Each of us a little a chunk of soul."

I wait in the quiet, then begin.

"There was a man named Cyrus Teed," I tell her. "He was a scientist and philosopher and claimed to have seen God as a woman robed in gold and purple. In the late 1800's he traveled America lecturing his ideas. He taught that God was both male and female, that matter and electricity were interchangeable, and that the earth was hollow."

"Ah ha," she breathes a laugh.

"But he had a twist. We, all humanity, everything we see, is on the inside. On the concave surface. If we could fly straight up we'd reach the other side of the world. If we were to dig down a hundred miles, we'd reach the empty void of space."

"Cool," she says, and I can hear her smile.

"Can you imagine giving up everything to journey into the earth's interior and discovering we've been here the whole time," I say, laughing a little. "My God, I hope there's something better than us at the center of all of this."

"Oliver," she says, her voice nearly a whisper. "Don't go back to the Agape Center, okay?"

I don't say a thing. I let her words float in the dark.

"You don't belong and I don't like seeing you there," she says, her voice slurred with sleep. "Go back to teaching."

"I've got nothing to teach."

"Do something. Go somewhere," she mumbles. "Go to the North Pole. Just do something."

"I don't have the money," I say. But that's not quite true.

Before long her breathing deepens and I know she is asleep. I lay a sheet over her.

I stay awake with her smell, cut flowers, and her breathing, tiny waves breaking on a soft shore. She dreams, her body moving slightly under the sheet and I am again perplexed as to her presence.

Ashley sleeps. I stay awake and remember.

My lawyer had prepared us as best he could. This wasn't a trial. Tom wasn't even going to be in the room. Just the judge, prosecuting lawyer, and a jury of our peers—a grand jury. They weren't deciding innocence or guilt, just whether there should be a trial.

We sat in the courtroom lobby—Tom, Carrie, and I—waiting to be called in.

"I'll be so glad when this is over and we can get back to our lives," Carrie said, her face round with new pregnant weight. Her eyes bright and terrified.

"Amen," said Tom.

Carrie wore a navy blue dress, her belly just beginning to bulge. She held my hand.

They called her first.

"This might take a while," Tom said. "Want a coffee or something?"

"What are they asking her?"

"What happened that night. How's your marriage. Are you stable."

I sighed.

"Oliver, I've told you, they don't have a case. You're fine. Still no cause of death. They don't even have a method. They've got a forensic toxicologist making guesses." He paused for beat. "They're just shooting in the dark."

"I understand."

"I'm not wild about the prosecutor. The smarmy bastard wants to make a name for himself." He said. "So you got a little tipsy. Spilled some scotch. It was Christmas Eve, for God's sake."

I nodded.

"You loved your son," he said, nodding to himself. "That's what counts."

For thirty-five minutes I sat with Tom. I opened up a magazine, but I had already began my non-reading days. When I looked up, Tom would catch my eye and smile. So I stopped looking up.

Finally she came out. I should have known then. Her face was new—older and drawn.

"So," Tom said, standing. "How'd it go?"

I stood, too. She glanced at me. Something had changed. Not tears, not grief. This was something new again. Her eyes never saw me that way before.

"I need to use the bathroom," she said and walked away.

Tom patted my back. "Your turn."

In the witness booth, they swore me in. I looked over the jury, curious to see if I knew any of them. But as it turned out, my peers were all strangers.

The prosecuting lawyer was handsome, almost charming. He asked me to recount the events of Christmas Eve and Christmas morning. I described the evening walk, the neighborhood party, leaving for the grocery store. I had repeated it so many times, it no longer felt that I was leaving anything out.

"And at what time did you leave to buy milk?"

"I'm not sure. Eleven or twelve."

"Odd time to make a run to the grocery store," he said, pacing the courtroom before me, smiling at me.

"I wanted us to have ingredients to make—"

"Pancakes. Yes, you said that." He paused, placing his palms together, an open-eyed prayer. "You say you left before twelve, yes?"

I nodded.

"But according to your credit card you didn't purchase anything until 2:16 AM on Christmas morning." He stared at me, silent for a moment.

"I could be wrong about the time."

His eyes brightened, as if the question was only now occurring to him. "Dr. Bonds, what were you doing for those two hours?"

I saw the faces of the jury, saw their muscles tense, foreheads crease.

"I don't know," I said. "Like I said, I may have had the time wrong."

"You had been drinking, correct?"

"Well, yes. Not much." I said. "We'd been at a party and—"

"Dr. Bonds, did you plan on having a child?" he asked, turning from me as he spoke.

"Yes. We both wanted a family."

"Wasn't your wife on birth control when she became pregnant with your son?"

"She still had a prescription, but we had stopped using it."

"Did you regret her pregnancy?"

"No," I said, sand in my throat. "I wanted to have a child."

"And you took life insurance for your baby. Is that correct?"

"Yes," I said, looking to the jury. "I took it out for all of us. It was package deal."

"So you were prepared for the possibility of your baby dying?" he asked.

"It wasn't like that."

"Were you happy as a married man, Dr. Bonds? As a father?"

"Yes," I said.

He nodded slowly. Then pointed to a flat screen television hanging on the wall of the courtroom.

"Can you tell me who this is?"

For a moment the screen buzzed black, then an image snapped into view—Ashley's naked body on the green couch. The picture she'd sent me that night.

"Do you know this woman?"

The image glared from the screen.

"Dr. Bonds?"

"Did you show this to Carrie?" I asked, hearing the pitifulness of the words as I spoke them.

"Please answer the question. Who is this woman?"

"I'd . . . rather not say."

"She's a student of yours, isn't she?"

"A former student," I said.

"Were you or are you having an affair with this woman?"

"No."

"You did not have sex with this woman?"

"I didn't."

"She just sent you a picture. Maybe for extra credit?"

A few snickers. Sick air in that room.

Now I looked at him. He was building a narrative. His story was better than mine. My version had no lesson, no moral. It made no sense and therefore floated like fluff. The handsome lawyer was offering a reason this had all happened. My God, how we wanted a reason.

"I didn't touch her." I said.

The lawyer paused and stared at the image of Ashley. With his stare he gave everyone permission to join him. Ashley on the couch. He clicked a button and there was Ashley, her pink towel falling. Ashley's legs. He turned back to me.

"Perhaps, Dr. Bonds, you no longer wanted to be a father."

SHE WAS GONE WHEN I CAME OUT OF THE COURTROOM.

Tom drove me home.

"How did they find those pictures?" I asked.

"You should have told me," he said. "I'm not judging you, but you should have told me."

"I didn't do anything." I said. "Where did they find them? I erased them."

"Nothings ever erased, Oliver," he said. "You know that."

I found Carrie in the nursery hanging moons and stars. The yellow had not mellowed. It screamed from the wall.

I watched her balancing on a stepstool, pressing red block letters to the wall: A R C H E R. Stepping off, she wobbled and I moved to steady her. She jerked away as if I'd burned her.

"Carrie."

"Don't."

She stood, her arms across her chest, her jaw biting tears back, the damn mobile spinning awkward above her head, and the yellow stabbing. Me, three feet away and unable to touch her.

"Oliver," she said, her eyes staring down. "I have to ask . . ."

I knew she would. I knew she had to. I had already run through answers in my head—*it was a girl with a crush. A flirtation. Nothing.*

But that wasn't the question.

"Did you do it . . ." she paused and everything that pulsed in me seized up. "Did you do anything to Miles?"

"Carrie," Her name stuck in me. "Carrie."

She looked up. Her eyes burrowing backwards, escaping like night crawlers after a storm.

My answer didn't matter. It didn't matter even if she believed me. She knew I was innocent. But it did not matter. Once she could conceive me as capable, we ended. The possibility that I had let our son die on purpose was poison so potent one drop fouled the whole cauldron. Every look would hold that possibility. Every touch gummy with that question.

She was always the bolder of us. The stronger. Not until she asked me that question had I dared to ask myself.

Solid as a rock, she and I.

We were dead.

I WAKE UP ON THE FLOOR. A BLANKET HAS BEEN DRAPED OVER ME. My back protests as I sit up. Ashley is still asleep in my bed, her mouth slightly ajar.

Everything feels strange. Not bad. Just strange.

I sneak into the bathroom and step into the shower. I stay there until the water turns cold and the pipes wheeze.

When I come out wrapped in a towel, the bed is empty. Though the shed's hardly bigger than a walk-in closet, I scan the room to see if she's still here.

"No, that's fine. Fine." Miller's slight brogue rings from outside. "He's lucky to have a friend like you."

He's answered by Ashley's scratchy laugh. Ashley talking to Miller.

Oh God. I jump to the door, but stop. I'm naked.

I look for my pants. Any pants. I root through the shed, looking under sheets. Through the thin wall they talk on in quieter tones. I've got one leg in and I'm falling to the floor. But that's okay, because I land on my shoes.

Two legs in, shirt half-buttoned, I throw open the door and Mr. Miller stands before me grinning.

"So, Oliver, you've got a girlfriend?"

"Mr. Miller. Good morning." I look past him, but see no one. She's gone.

"She's a winner, Oliver. A real beauty."

"Just a friend."

"Just a friend, eh? Then you might want to buckle your pants."

I fumble with my zipper and Miller chuckles. His good humor is disconcerting.

"So is she moving in, or just paying the rent?"

He's examining a check in his hand.

"What is that?" I grab the check from him.

"Looks like you've got a sugar mama, Oliver, you lucky bastard. Now you still owe me back rent for— What the hell are you doing?"

I rip away and the shreds of check fall from my hands like winter leaves.

I push by him and down the steps.

"You can't live like this, Oliver."

I look for her car. But I don't even know what she drives.

"You've got to grow up."

I turn and stare at Miller, standing with his arms out like a welcoming Virgin Mary.

"I know it's been a rough patch. God knows I know. But that's not an excuse to lose your mind. Not an excuse to piss away a helping hand."

"I'll get you the rent."

"Fuck, Oliver, do you really think I need a couple of hundred dollars that bad?" He drops his arms and furrows his brow. "Well, I probably do. But that's not why I'm standing lecturing you like some goddamn Sunday school teacher." He runs a hand where his hair used to be. Then points at me, punctuating each word with a jab. "I used to drink, Oliver. Drank my weight and more most nights. I was the cliché, a drunk Irish man getting into fights with hicks at the Horseshoe Lounge. Until my wife said if I don't stop, she leaves. Even then I didn't stop. She left me, Oliver. She left for a month. And I got so drunk I was sick on myself. Pissed like the Pope on Easter." He nods, quick flicks of his chin. "I cleaned up. Hard as all fuck. Still is. Hard as all fuck, but better."

He shakes his head and a pained smile crosses his face for an instant.

"Oliver," he says, eyes on mine. "The path of least resistance leads to nothing but shit."

"I'll get your money. I don't need hers." I turn and walk back into the shed.

"You're forcing my hand, Oliver," he yells after me. "You are forcing my hand."

I stand in the shed, my clothes clinging to my wet body. I don't want her money. I don't want his advice. Miles left us fifty thousand that I've never touched. Maybe Ashley is right. Maybe it's time to act, no matter the cost.

I KNOCK ON LYLE'S DOOR UNTIL HE ANSWERS WEARING NOTHING BUT white underwear well past their expiration date.

"I shouldn't be awake right now," he says, putting a cigarette into his mouth and striking his lighter. "It's not healthy."

He turns and I follow him inside. He pulls on a shirt, somehow managing to continue smoking the entire time.

"I worked a double yesterday," he says. "I thought if we hand Horner some cash along with the Visa check, maybe Horner would let it slide. But I made less than a hundred."

Lyle's apartment is draped with white Christmas lights and always smells of bacon grease. He owns one luxury item, an oversized red velvet couch that he inherited from a roommate who skipped town years before. The apartment is a constant mess—dirty dishes, empty bottles. But the couch is pristine thanks to the clear, plastic covering that incases it like a body bag. I sit on the couch, the plastic squeaking.

"But I've been thinking," he says, pulling on his pants. "We need to hit up the Hollow Earth Society. Just a couple thousand from each of them, and we're on our way."

"I have the money," I say. "All of it."

"No, you don't."

"We had a life insurance policy on my son. It's fifty thousand dollars."

He pauses, his pants unbuckled. "You have 50k in the bank?"

I nod.

"You have 50k in the bank and you eat breakfast at a homeless shelter?"

"I've never touched the money."

"I sold sperm twice this week and you have fifty thousand dollars?"

"That I couldn't spend, yes."

"So what changed?"

"If you don't hear a heartbeat, go looking for the heart. I want to know if the core of all, all of this, is good or evil or just plain apathetic. I need to see the center. I want an answer."

Lyle stares at me for a long moment. "You want to know how your son died."

I shake my head. "I want to know why he died."

"Okay." He rubs his cheeks. "The bank opens at nine. Let's eat waffles first." He picks up his car keys. "You're buying."

I don't feel good here at all. The place is designed for money and those who have it. It's in the grey and black color scheme, the low, cushioned furniture, the perfect knots of the employee's ties, even the sliding doors seem to whisper *cash*. Everything reminds me that Lyle and I are not welcome here.

But there's more. It's the money waiting in my account. The fifty thousand. The sum that so many believed motivated me to kill my son. Walking in I glance at the security guard with a gun holstered to his side. He looks back and I quickly put eyes to the floor.

Lyle strides to the counter, oblivious to any inhospitality. He addresses a young man behind the counter.

"I represent Dr. Oliver Bonds. We'd like to withdraw twenty thousand dollars."

I feel suddenly frightened. I expect someone to point at me, someone to yell, *He finally came for the money. He waited until he thought we'd forgotten. Grab him.*

The young man smiles. "Have you got an account with us?"

"I don't," Lyle says and points at me. "He does."

"All right. I'll need your social security number and a valid ID."

I watch him type in my information. What does his screen say?

Does it tell him where the money came from? Does it have a link to the news articles and comment threads calling for my death?

I look back to the security guard, who catches my eye and nods unsmiling.

"Oh, hum." The young man frowns. It's a trap. This is all a trap. "There's currently a hundred and fourteen dollars in this account."

"I don't understand," I say.

"Me either," Lyle says.

"I'm sorry, Mr. Bonds." He keeps glancing at his countertop computer. "The account hasn't had any movement in over a year. It was a shared account with you and your wife."

"Ex-wife," I say. What does it say about her? What does it say about our marriage?

"It looks like most of the money was transferred to another account?"

"Whose account?" Lyle says. He's too loud. We shouldn't be here.

"May I suggest you contact Carrie Bonds?" he says.

"Ah, Jesus," Lyle exclaims. "The whiz kid wants to play marriage counselor. Look, sometimes relationships end."

"No, I just meant . . ."

"I haven't her seen in years," I say, my voice sounds weak.

"Would you like to close the account?" he asks.

"Please don't make me go to her," I say.

"Sir, I —"

"I have to go see her, don't I?" I ask him. He looks at me blankly, his mouth ajar. I know I make no sense. I'm asking things he can't answer, but who else am I going to ask?

I turn to Lyle, shaking my head. He stares back without sympathy.

"We are going to see her, Ollie. We're going right now."

Last time I saw Carrie was across a table at a grocery store coffee shop. She handed me legal papers to sign and end our marriage. We had made it, at least on paper, as long as the criminal case stood.

We waited for months. I wanted a trial. I fantasized about speaking my part, sharing my side, letting the truth convince the jury, the judge, and, most importantly, Carrie that I was innocent and undeserving of all this pain. I wanted the truth to battle the narrative. But the grand jury said there was not enough evidence to warrant a trial. I was not pronounced *innocent*. Not even *not guilty*. The case just ended. No indictment. The papers published small pieces using loose terms like "technicality" and "undetermined."

No day in court. No answer. No reason.

The final description of Miles's death was Sudden Unexplained Death in Childhood. Every year over two hundred toddlers die this way. We call it SUDC, but that simply means we have no idea.

My case sputtered and ended. No victory. No defeat.

Once the case was over, so was any last thread of commitment between Carrie and me. I signed the papers and handed them back.

"How's Manuel," I asked.

"Fine," she said, stacking the papers neatly.

She picked up her purse to leave, then stopped and looked me. "How many?"

"How many what?" I asked.

"How many students did you have sex with?" she frowned. "I just feel it's fair for me to know."

What could I tell her? What was kinder? All she wanted was a storyline with beats and understandable consequences. I wanted to lie, to tell her there were dozens of lovers, that I was never true, that our marriage had been a sham and she was lucky to be free. Painful as the story was, it was preferable to randomness.

I shook my head and said nothing. She pushed her chair back and left me sitting there alone.

I direct Lyle south of town to a safe, well-groomed pastel suburb. I know exactly where she lives. He pulls up in front of a house looking like a series of boxes elegantly stacked. The lawn green, the paint earth red, the door blue, the windows a reflecting shine you can't see past. This is Manuel's house. We used to come over as a family. Now she is his wife and his home is her home.

I tell Lyle to wait in the car. He tries to argue, but I refuse to let him leave the car.

"Don't let her give you the run around, okay Ollie?"

I walk the long path to the heavy, engraved wooded door—like an old church. I'm terrified. I knock. Wait.

A girl, maybe ten years old, answers the door. Manuel's daughter.

"Is Carrie here?"

"She's . . ." She frowns. ". . . in the bathroom."

"I can wait."

"It won't take long."

"Mamma going poop!" A boy runs in the background.

The girl cringes. "He just likes that word. I'm pretty sure it's just number one."

The boy gallops to her side. I know him. I know his blonde hair and quick eyes. It's Archer.

"Mamma going poop," he cheers again. He stands wavering, his squat two-year-old body working to balance itself.

The boy tumbles toward me and grabs my leg. He stares up into my face. He has his mother's face, but not her hair.

I don't move. I don't smile. The girl starts to peel him off, apologizing. But the boy clings, singing out the news of his mother's bowel movement.

"Oliver?" Carrie arrives at the door. She's older. Of course she is. She's beautiful. She's wearing a white summer dress. Her auburn hair is down, pushed to one side.

She doesn't like seeing me.

"Sorry, Mom. Archer's doing that thing again."

"Katie, will you take him upstairs?"

She hefts the boy up in her arms and awkwardly lugs him back into the house and out of sight. I watch him go until Carrie puts her body in the doorframe, blocking my view.

She really doesn't like seeing me.

"Hi Carrie."

"Oliver. I didn't expect you."

"You look good."

"Do you need something?"

"I see him playing at the daycare. I watch him play."

Her jaw tightens.

"How are you doing?" I ask, and it feels so strange.

"This isn't the best time. Katie has a volleyball game."

"Our account is empty."

She pauses, crosses her arms and nods.

"Yes." She nods. "I tried calling, but your phone—"

"I don't have one," I say.

"Manuel should be home soon. Can you come back later and we can discuss this then?"

"My friend is waiting."

She runs a hand through her hair. Some of the shine has faded, it's a slightly different color. She wouldn't know. Too gradual to notice.

But I haven't seen her in two and a half years. I no longer get to see her change.

"It wasn't healthy to leave the money sitting there. So we used it. Mainly for the house. And his daughter. My daughter now. Katie has braces."

"I need some of the money," I say.

"I'm sure we can come to some kind of arrangement." She presses her brow, an old habit. "Are you working these days?"

"I'm going to the North Pole. There's a hole there that leads into the earth. I can explain the science behind it if you'd like. But it all comes down to needing that money."

"To go to the North Pole?"

"Past the Pole, into the Earth. There's a hole."

She stares at me, and it hurts. A puzzled, angry look.

"I've been selected for an expedition," I say.

She shakes her head and looks at me again, familiar creases bridging her eyes. And something new, a look I don't recognize. Something disappointed and angry and sad.

"The money is gone," she says.

"It wasn't your money," I say. "Miles was my son, too."

She flinches when I say his name.

"Even if I had . . ." she starts, but falters. "I would not allow you to spend his money this way."

"Instead of vinyl siding for your new husband's house? Or braces?"

"That's not fair." She glances back and then leans forward, whispering. "You've never paid child support. Not a dime. I could have you arrested."

"For Archer?"

"Yes, for Archer," she says, her eyes cutting at me.

"Does he need anything?"

She shakes her head. "That's not the point."

"Archer's a good name." I say. She looks at me, a new kind of surprised.

"Oliver, you named him."

I stare.

"You always said if we had another boy we would name him Archer."

"Yes, but . . ." I move my head and watch my hands twitch. Something shakes in me. I try and breathe it down but I can't.

"Are you all right?" she asks.

"The two massive holes in our earth, the Symmes Holes, are named for Captain John Cleves Symmes."

"Oliver."

"When he was a young officer, he was in a duel. A bullet ripped through his gut and out his back. A hole all the way through." I hear my voice, strange and cracked, and I see her face cringe. "He theorized that the earth must have as thorough a wound."

"Oliver, stop," she says, her voice something like afraid. "The money is gone."

"Don't you see, Carrie, our lives are crust until something cracks them open. Then you can look inside. But you've moved as far away from the edge as you can, you won't even peek."

"I'm closing the door," she says.

"You won't even look inside."

"You need to leave, Oliver."

"I miss you so much, Carrie. I miss you so very much."

But the door is already closed.

THE THING THAT HAD BEGUN TO SHAKE IN ME CONTINUES. LYLE urges me away from Carrie's door, he ushers me to the car, and drives us into the city. He assures me it will be okay, shooting side-glances at me as I watch the city, the skyline shaking.

Miles's money does not exist. There's no way in. And Carrie is completely gone. She's been gone for years, but it was only when she was looking at me, blocking her children from me, staring with disgust—how dare I fall when she has propped herself up from every angle—only then did I know how completely I have lost her.

I'm whispering as we drive and it takes me some minutes before I understand that I'm trying to pray.

As a boy, I used to pray. As a grown man, I was wiser. I'd sit alone or with Carrie in the pews of St. Christopher, bowing my head and reciting the words. But I knew better. I had, I felt, a mind that was able to both believe and not believe. I could say, "Father in Heaven" and know I didn't believe in any divine Parent in any mythical Heaven. I could enjoy the prayers as metaphors.

I spent hours thinking how I could say God's name without believing in God—at least not the simple father-figure, sky-king God of the masses. Every time I said, "Our Father," I mentally substituted more acceptable, more sophisticated concepts of the Divine.

But when I hurt, I screamed for God. When my mother died, during my wife's long labor, and when I clutched Miles's unmoving body from his crib. I screamed silent prayers—I prayed as if a person were listening. All my intellectual acrobatics revealed themselves to be a child's attempt to recite a parent's DNA code instead of calling for his mother. I wanted to think of God not as a Person but as a Source. A Force. But you can't scream at the Ground of All Being. It's like trying to kiss the ocean. A certain degree of intimacy is easier if all involved have faces.

Even with faces, you can lose each other. I lost Carrie. I lost her. She was looking at me and I could not understand her.

I cannot pray. I cannot call out. Even as everything in me shakes.

Lyle steers us into the Book Spot parking lot.

"So we don't have all the money," Lyle says, more to himself than to me. "We've got the Visa check. That's a good start."

Lyle barely has the car parked before he's leaping from the seat.

"Remember," he's telling me. "You're blind."

He's pulling me along toward the front doors. I feel weak, uninterested. I'm trying to remember being excited, being thrilled. But there's nothing.

Horner's face, glossy and annotated, greets us as we enter the bookstore. It's positioned on a poster resting on an aisle just inside the sliding door.

"Has it started yet?" Lyle breathlessly asks a plump, bearded guy re-stocking the serial killer shelf in the True Crime section.

"Has what started yet?"

But Lyle hasn't waited for an answer. He's dragging me to the back of the store, zig-zagging through aisles of books. We turn a corner into a self-help aisle and standing there ¬short, with gray around the sideburns, tiny capillaries spidering along his cheeks, a thick mustache and brown felt fedora—is Dr. Jim Horner.

He's going through some notes with a bored looking woman in a Book Spot staff shirt. Just beyond him in an open area is a small crowd seated in folding chairs. He looks to us and Lyle freezes, his hand still clutching my arm.

"Here for the reading?" Horner asks, his voice is familiar from his podcasts.

"Dr. Horner," Lyle seems to hic-up out of his paralysis. "I'm a devotee. It is a true honor to meet you. I'm Lyle Burn—"

"Lyle Burnside," Dr. Horner says, gripping Lyle's free hand and matching his enthusiasm. "You're joining us on the expedition."

"Yes, yes, that's right," Lyle says, nodding like a puppy.

"And this must be Professor Bonds." He reaches for my hand hanging at my side and takes it in both of his. I look toward him and blink. He smiles. "I'm hoping the audio version of this book will be complete before we set sail."

"I'll read it to him!" Lyle nearly squeals. "It's my job."

I feel confused by all of this, on stage with the wrong script.

"By the way, sir," Lyle digs into his back pocket and retrieves a folded Visa check. "It's only five thousand, but the rest is coming."

Horner pockets the check without glancing at the number. "Excellent. It's our pooled talents, money, and faith that fuel this expedition."

Lyle grins and turns to the chairs, nearly forgetting me. He quickly catches himself and takes hold of my arm again. I stumble a little as he pulls me away, knocking my leg against one of the dozen folding chairs set out for the event.

"Don't over do it," Lyle whispers.

Ten or so people sit scattered among the chairs. Belinda, Bentley, and the others from the Hollow Earth Society are out in full force. The bored employee steps behind the podium and begins reading into the unnecessary microphone.

"This evening we are honored to have with us notable scientist and writer of several world-rattling books . . ." She pauses and glances to the side where Horner stands, grinning, nodding for her to continue. "He's an adventurer, internet radio host, and critically-acclaimed poet . . ." She stops again and looks up at us, deadpan, questioning if we are actually serious. Seeing that we are, she sighs and continues. "Here to read from his new book *Our Journey In* is Dr. Jim Horner."

People clap. Lyle hoots. Dr. Horner swaggers up to the podium. What are we doing here? My foot taps the linoleum floor.

"Thank you for that kind introduction, ma'am. You must have read my FBI file," Dr. Horner says to the retreating back of the employee. The crowd laughs. "It's good to be back in Texas. Texas, I get. Texas, I like. Hell, you were your own country. Who knows, maybe you will be again."

I tap, tap, tap. I see Lyle, his face shinning. I see Belinda, her hands folded neatly in her lap, swaying to these words. And I imagine Carrie looking at me. My god, look at me.

"There's a honeycomb of deception our country has constructed to hide the truth of the inner earth. Secret expeditions, censoring of Admiral Byrd, and the true mission of NASA. I'll give you a hint. It ain't space . . ."

He opens his book and reads and we sit enraptured. And I tap, tap.

". . . in the heart of the Hollow Earth is a massive mirror or screen on which our enlightened inner earth cousins monitor our progress . . ."

It's just another narrative. Just another story that's easier than the obvious.

"This mirror holds the answers to our deepest whys."

Tap. Tap. I can't stop.

Every other moment, I'm not sure the world is still below me and my foot reaches out to touch. The same way I woke every ten minutes that first night in the hospital to check on Miles in his crib. To touch and believe. To touch and assure.

Tapping. Always tapping. Not only to affirm that the world, but that I am there. I spent my adult life acquiring accolades to try and convince myself I existed. Degrees, relationships, jobs. Tapping.

From orgasms to tenure—all so I could tap the earth and believe I existed. Everything I have ever done accumulates to nothing more than tapping.

"People," Horner reads. "We are on the verge of the next Copernican revolution. Every history, science, and philosophy textbook will have to be rewritten. Heroes will be exposed as liars. And the disenfranchised will be honored as extraordinary."

I still feel Carrie's eyes condemning me. Maybe she's as lost as I am, but she lives in a real house, and she cares for children.

Why did I believe there was some place to journey to? The ground is cold beneath my feet. Maybe God was once there, maybe the earth held secrets and wisdom, but it's all frozen now.

"It's stone." I say it under my breath. Lyle glances at me.

"And we, we here today," Dr. Horner says, his eyes touching each of us. "We will have helped to deliver humanity through a new birth into a new era."

"It is stone," I say loudly. Bentley and a few others turn in their seats.

"We are the midwives," Horner continues. "We are—"

"It is stone!" I yell.

Horner stops. Now everyone is looking and I stand.

"There is nothing but rock and ice and graves below us. Ice and stone."

Belinda opens her mouth but says nothing.

"Professor?" Dr. Horner says.

I jump up and land hard, slamming my feet against the floor.

"See?"

I do it again. Jumping as high as I can and slamming my legs down.

"No echo," I say. "Nothing but solid nothing."

"Jesus, Ollie, what are you doing?" Lyle says, reaching out to me.

I swipe away his hand. "This guy is lying to you, Lyle. There's no hole. There's no window into the mind of god. There's nothing. He's a liar and you as a liar should know that."

"Professor Bonds, please," Horner says. I turn and step straight toward him. He cowers a little behind the podium, but holds his ground.

"And you!" I say, pointing. "There will be no new birth. There will be no discovery." I turn to the small crowd. "You want something new, but there's nothing new. Nothing is going to change."

The big guy from True Crime grabs my shoulder. I shake him off and leap on to a folding chair, which immediately collapses. I tumble forward, entangled in a mesh of metal and plastic.

I lay there twisting, swatting out at anyone who comes close to me. Standing at a distance, I see Lyle with an expression I've never seen on his face before. I've hurt him. I didn't know I could.

The True Crime guy hauls me to my feet.

"Be careful," Horner calls out as I'm pulled away. "He's blind."

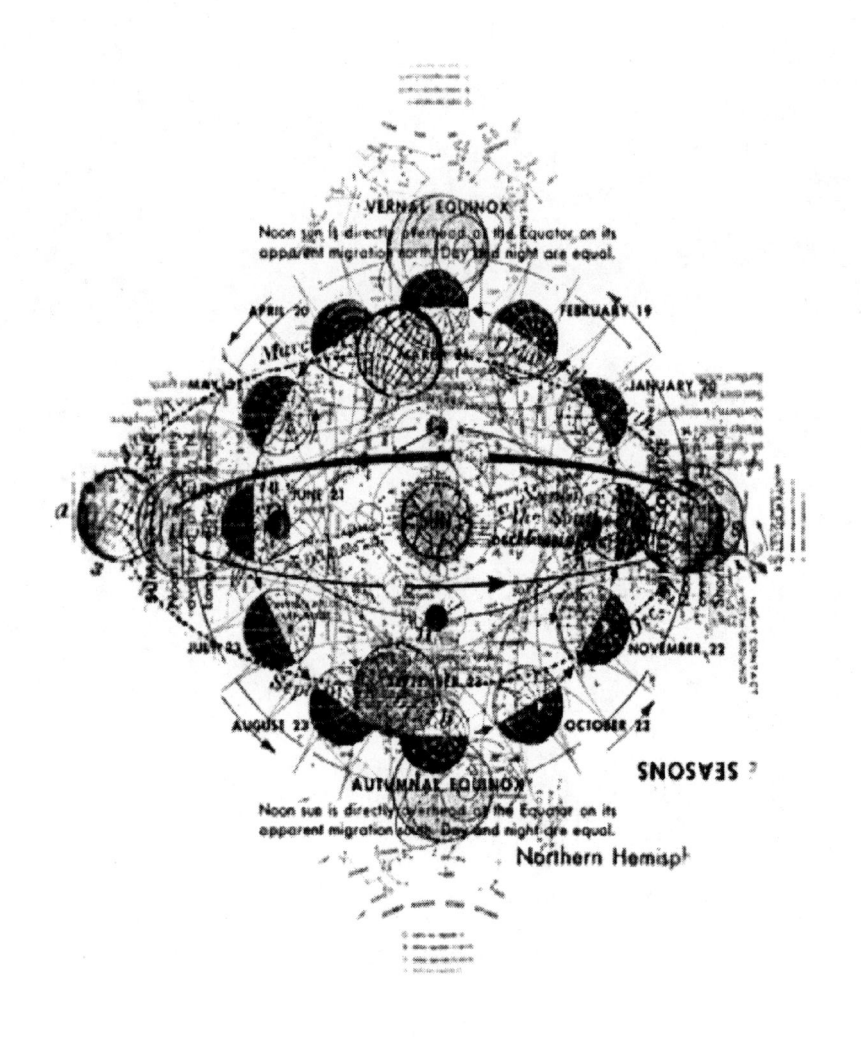

WHIRLPOOL

The tremendous swells would heave us up to the very peaks of mountainous waves, then plunge us down into the depths of the sea's trough as if our fishing-sloop were a fragile shell. —Olaf Jansen

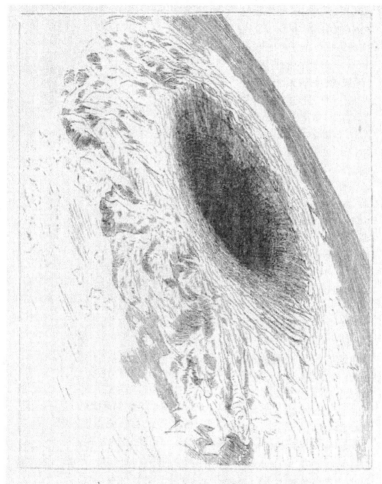

SYMMES'S HOLE, AS IT WOULD APPEAR TO A LUNARIAN WITH A TELESCOPE.

THE DAYROOM IS A SLOW HELL, PISS-SCENTED AND FLUORESCENT, furnished like a cheap university study room. This is the Austin State Hospital. Known as A.S.H. or Ash. They brought me here yesterday. The admitting lobby smelled dank and singed, an over-taxed heater wheezed somewhere above us.

Paperwork was filed, passed through plastic-glass windows to unsmiling admittance staff. Then waiting. More papers. Waiting, feet tapping linoleum floors. I recognize this dance—the police station, hospitals, courtrooms.

They took my shoes, afraid I'd use the laces to kill myself, and I was given a pair of olive green plastic sandals. Almost immediately I was medicated, a jellybean-sized pill that turned the storm into clouds, rain into fog, and left me dull and lost. I slept without dreams and without true rest, like floating on top of water, unable to sink beneath the surface.

This morning they lead me to the dayroom. Two dozen or so patients fill the space, some sit bent and staring like bad-posture Buddhas. Others conspire in corners, argue over board games, hide in year-old magazines. Still others scream. A woman stands by the water fountain crying, a puddle of pee forming at her feet. An older man with fiery eyes keeps calling the name of a nurse and rubbing his crotch. No one pays any attention till the cock pops free and nurses step from their station, warning him to "Put it away, Mr. Bilton."

A television plays a ceaseless line of crime and cops, the dialogue echoing off the walls and blurring into nonsense. A woman keeps knocking on the nurses' window yelling that her son is supposed to pick her up. "He's supposed to be here. Can you check? Can you see if he's here? Can I just peek outside and see?"

I've seen one doctor. Dr. Bradley, a balding man who kept his eyes on my file. "So, had a little brouhaha at the bookstore. Why was that?"

"I realized the earth is solid."

He hummed. "Is that so bad, Mr. Bonds?"

I shook my head. "It means that what you see is what you get."

"I'm going to recommend lorazepam and set you up for observation. We'll have you here for a week or two."

"I don't need to be here."

He pulled a stapled stack of papers from my file. "What do you think about signing yourself in?" He shrugged. "Or I can sign, either way."

"Contact Ashley Briggers. She's a caseworker at the Agape Resource Center. I don't need to be here."

"Oh, now, Mr. Bonds." He scribbled a signature on the papers. "No one is here by accident."

In the dayroom a girl hollers into a corner so endlessly I can taste the blood in the air from her excoriated throat. A big man with forehead veins says I can wear his watch—a faux-gold wristwatch. I can wear it for one hour. I refuse the offer. The veins pulse, he shakes his head.

"You should really wear the watch, man."

I say no and he walks away, glancing back at me again and again.

Two orderlies with wrestling-thick arms and shiny eyes talk near the nurses' station.

"They've got their own cemetery here, did you know that?" says one. "It's over on North Loop between the condos."

"People buried there?"

"Hundreds, maybe thousands. But no one knows about it. No gravestones. A few have patient numbers, but most are just dumped, buried one on top of the other."

"Shit," says the other. "I'd hate to be buried there."

"What would you care? You'd be dead."

"I'd care."

Meals are saltless and lukewarm, followed by more jellybean pills. Then more waiting, more funk and whine. All these people— groaning and speechless and near-nameless. All these shuffling med-heads in a fog so thick they're drowning on their feet.

The nurses say little. "Less chatter people. More eating." "Big swig of water. Swallow it all." They keep to their glass shark cage, stepping out only to again order Mr. Bilton's cock back in his pants.

This was here. These people were always here. I lived my life— restaurants and movies and cocktails and books and all the while these people were here. How could I have been happy? How can any life be good when this hell is here?

We sleep four to a room. My bed is the bottom bunk in the corner. Lights-out brings a murmur of whimpering and masturbating like the horrid hum of overgrown insects. And that singed heater rattles from the ceiling. I cling to a pillow stinking of bleach and not quite dry laundry.

I turn to the wall, my eyes unclosing. The paint on the concrete peels back a little. I touch the wall, it's cool. I pick at the paint, peeling it back. It crumbles under my finger like dry clay. I peel more away, making a dark hole in the wall.

"Hey." Someone's kneeling by my bed. "Hey, let me crawl in with you."

"No," I say.

"Come on. Let me crawl in with you."

"Get off my bunk."

It's the big man with the watch.

"Don't be like that," he says. "You don't have to do anything. I'll do it all. Come on."

"No."

"I'm going to put my hand over your mouth, but I don't want you to be scared."

His hand covers my mouth. I kick. I bite. He lets out a snicker.

"Squirming!" He sings. "Squirming Herman!"

The door swings open, the lights flicker on and an orderly barks.

"Back in your bunk, Cline. You leave him alone."

The orderly shakes his head and turns off the light.

I sit the dark, my legs tense and ready to kick, my hands ready to scratch. I look back at the hole I've made in the wall and an eye— round and albino—stares back. It blinks at me and I want to scream, but I can't seem to make a sound.

I hear the scratching from behind the wall. One long, slow scratch. The eye, translucent and piercing, stares. Now there's more scratching coming from the floor under my bunk. A slow chorus of a dozen claws scrapping beneath the floorboards. I look back at the eye. It's not human.

Are these the nameless corpses? Have they wormed their way from their graves to here? I called the earth solid, but listen to the scratching. Listen to gurgled cries just below the floor.

The eye moves from the hole and for a moment there's only black. Then a long, trollish finger with loose grey, skin extends from the darkness. It comes slowly, but I cannot move. The jagged, white nail at the tip of the finger scratches along my arm and even now, I cannot move.

"Squirming Herman," the big man whispers from across the room. "Squirming Herman. Don't go to sleep."

There are those that teach that the creatures inhabiting the hollow earth are demonic, devolved things moving blindly beneath us, stealing the nameless, the homeless, the ones no one will miss. They pull them beneath and feed their young.

The grey finger runs down to my wrist. I try to pull away, but I'm frozen. They will take me if I don't move. They will wrap me in this urine soaked mattress and pull me below the floor, through the dirt, and into the cave-riddled crust. I strain, urging my body to act. Finally, like breaking from a dream that holds just past waking, I move. I jerk away and the finger retreats into the hole. The eye returns, blinking at me. I jab my finger at it, feeling the soft, wet of the eye. Behind the wall I hear the muffled, trollish cry, and I stuff my pillow into the hole.

I won't scream. I won't. If I do, the orderlies will strap me down or drug me to sleep and these demons will eat me. I'll sit and keep watch till morning. They can't stand the day. The sun is poison.

"Squirming Herman," the big man sings to himself.

I see it now. I understand now. The earth is not stone. It's Hell all the way through.

THE DAYROOM COUCH SAGS. OUTSIDE THE SKY ROLLS DISHWATER gray. They've let me use the phone twice. I've tried to call Lyle and warn him, but no one answers. The pills make everything slower, tamer. The couch could catch fire and I'd only yawn.

The woman calling for her son is back at the nurses' station. The nurse on duty keeps her eyes on her paperwork, bureaucracy like gloves. I rise and walk to her.

"I'm Oliver," I say.

"I think they've kidnapped him," she says.

"Your son."

"That woman right there." She point through the glass at the nurse, who is now answering a blinking phone. "My son came to visit and they grabbed him."

"I'm so sorry."

"And his wife, too. Or she helped. She might have helped them."

"I hope not."

"They kidnap people every day. Every day. Then send them to England."

"Why England?" I ask. She looks at me like I'm crazy. Which, in my present condition, makes a lot of sense.

"For the Queen," she says. "*She's* the one in charge."

A small fist knocks from the other side of the window. The nurse stares through.

"Mr. Bonds," she says through the glass. "You're being released."

The mother looks at me with suspicion. "I said too much," she says, backing away.

I follow the orderly as he saunters down the long, beige hallway, his back bulging against his white uniform. I pad along, my olive-green sandals slapping the linoleum.

"You got a lady here to pick you up," he says. "Pretty one, too."

"She's my caseworker."

"Nice of her to come get you," he says. "Plenty people come in for three days, get a slap on the back and a day bus pass."

The drugs are still in my system making the lights hum a little too loudly.

But when he pushes through the last door and I walk in the admittance lobby, Ashley isn't there. My wife is.

"Hello, Oliver."

"Carrie. I . . ."

I glance at the orderly who smiles at me. "You do your best to stay on out of here, okay?" He turns and walks back out the door.

"Manuel is talking with your doctor," Carrie says. "How are you?"

"Did they call you?"

"Manuel's brother-in-law is on the board. Everything is worked out."

The door I just came through opens and out walks Manuel and Dr. Bradley laughing. Manuel dips his chin at Carrie, a couple's code, *everything is fine.* I hear her breathe out.

Manuel shakes my hand. "How are you feeling?"

I nod as an answer.

Dr. Bradley pats my back. "Take care of yourself, Dr. Bonds."

I ride in the backseat. Manuel and Carrie sit up front, sharing glances like concerned parents. Outside my window I see geese in the gray sky.

"I didn't know how bad things were, Oliver," Carrie says, turning in her seat. "You should have said."

"I need to find my friend Lyle," I say. "Could you drop me at his place?"

"Manuel and I talked," she says. "We're sorry about the money in the account. We should have had a conversation with you and not just presumed . . . "She trails off. Her brow wrinkles. It's hard for her to look at me. "I talked you your caseworker. She called and told us where you were."

"Ashley? You talked to her?"

"We want to help you get back on your feet, Oliver," Manuel says, slowing for a yellow light. "I have a cashiers check in my wallet for fifty-five hundred dollars. It's for you."

"We want to help," Carrie says.

"But we have to agree on some things," Manuel says, glancing at me in the rearview mirror. "This money is conditional."

"Conditional?"

"Listen, Oliver, I want to give you this check, but you've got to make some changes," Manuel says. "I have a friend who's a psychiatrist. She goes to St. Christopher's, too." The light turns green and the car inches forward. "I made an appointment for tomorr—Jesus, Oliver!"

I step out of the car, stumbling on the road.

"Oh God!" Carrie yelps.

I walk through the intersection. Cars dodge me.

"Oliver!" Manuel stands by the open driver's door. "You're going to get yourself killed."

"Chances are," I whisper.

I walk the mile through downtown to the Agape Center. Thick, hot air covers everything in a damp film. Inside, it's crowded and as humid with human sweat as it is outside with oncoming rain.

I want to talk to Ashley. Find out what she told Carrie. She's in her office nodding and listening to a crying mother holding a child.

I pace the room. They're talking politics in the back corner. They're arguing movies near the front. One man tries to play the piano, but a woman using the phones shuts him down. The scrap remains of breakfast—peels and crusts—fill the paper boats. Outside others are waiting to get in.

At a table near the door, a man sits in his wheelchair, his chin doubled upon itself as he slumps, his face wet from the morning rain, his eyes glassy and dull. How he survives, I have no idea.

A spot opens up on the computer and I sit, ready to write Lyle..

I have one unread email. It's a response from God. The thread of our conversation reads solid against the white screen:

> **Dear Oliver**
> **I dare you to take justice into your own hands. You know what you deserve. Now do it.**
> **God, your Eternal Father**

> **I will if You will.**
> **Oliver**

And finally God's reply. One word:

> **Deal.**

I stand, grab the monitor, and drop it on the floor. It makes a satisfying crunch. Chip the security guard is moving towards me but I stomp toward Charlie.

"Tell me your theology, Charlie," I say.

"Oliver . . ." he says, stepping back.

"You build it around the blazing son of God. A perfect man and his perfect suffering. Build it around him." I point to the drooling man in the wheelchair. "Build a theology around him, Charlie. What does that creation tell us about the Creator, Charlie?"

"Oliver, you have to calm down, or—"

"He does not care, so I say. He murders both the pure and the wicked."

Chip's hand grips my shoulder. "Come on, now. Oliver." He pushes me to the door. Miriam watches from her office door mad or amused or something.

"Charlie. I'm quoting scripture, Charlie!" I yell. *"You smear my wounds with ignorance."*

And then I'm outside. The rain dripping slow and the air too warm and thick.

"I have to ban you for a week," Chip says. He places his hands just above his security guard utility belt with pepper spray and an empty gun holster. "One week. Okay Oliver?"

I move back and my foot slips on the first steps. I stumble, falling down three steps and landing on my back.

I'm sitting on the curb when Ashley comes out. She sits beside me and for a long time neither of us say a word. The sky shifts and a drizzle begins.

"You talked to my wife," I say.

"I told her where you were."

"What if she'd recognized you? She's seen pictures."

"It was on the phone and I was fully dressed." She smiles. I can't bring myself to smile back.

"You freaked some people out in there," she says. "Gave quite the sermon."

"Would you like to know the key verse in Job?" I ask. "The lynchpin."

She hums.

"Job 13:15. *Though He slay me, yet I will trust in Him,*" I say.

"I know that one."

"The language is ambiguous. Perhaps intentionally. The same verse can just as likely be translated as *He kills me. I have no hope.*"

"Which one is it?" she asks.

I shake my head. "Either way, he slays us."

"You know, Oliver, you should have just fucked me. Then you'd have something to feel guilty about."

I look at her.

"People here have all kinds of problems. Handicaps, addiction, poverty. You're just sad. Not clinical depressed or chemically unbalanced. Just very sad." She meets my eyes. "You need to move on."

She blows out a breath and looks back at the street and the slowly forming puddles.

"You were a good teacher, you know that?" she says. "Now I'm going to teach you something. You're banned from Agape."

"I know. For a week."

"For life," she says. "You're not allowed to come back here."

I look at her, but she keeps her eyes on the passing cars.

"I've already cleared it with the staff. Chip has been told. If you show up, the police will be called."

"I'm sorry I broke the computer," I say.

She smiles and stands, brushing her pants. "I should get back to work."

I stand. "Why are you doing this?"

She turns and looks at me.

"Because I think I love you very much and I never want to see you again."

She walks through the center door and it closes behind her.

It rains on Austin. Hot rain that steams as it hits the blacktop roads and tin roofs and fills the street gutters with oak leaves and pollen.

I make my way back to my shed and find a new padlock gleaming on the door. The back window is clamped shut. He's left a note.

Oliver—You left me no choice. I'm hoping for the best for you. I really am.
                                        Michael Miller

I want to burn the whole place down. I want to watch it burn. He has no choice.

I hole up in the Whataburger on South First, sipping coffee and watching the parking lot puddles join and separate like continents of water.

They say the young earth's surface was all land once. Then came rivers and shallow seas, but no oceans. But as the earth expanded, the hollow within growing like a bubble, the land cracked apart and water filled the chasms. If we were able to *deflate* the globe, the continents would fit together like a sphere-shaped jigsaw.

At a payphone, I call Lyle's number again and again. A full voice-mail.

It's hours later and a short Hispanic man in an orange Whataburger uniform is asking me to leave.

"Why?" I ask.

"You're sleeping."

"I'm praying."

"Then find a church."

"Can I have more coffee?" I ask.

"No."

"The sign says bottomless."

"You've hit the bottom of a bottomless cup."

"That's discrimination."

"Oh no. Are you saying I've lost you as a customer? That's a hundred and thirty-five cents Whataburger will never see again."

"You're being sarcastic."

"Just leave before I call the cops."

I step outside, into the rain, and head downtown, searching for Lyle. I haven't seen him since the bookstore, since I saw that hurt in his eyes. He'll be working tonight, pedicabbing drunks from bar to bar to car.

The rain slows to a drizzle as the day ends. On Sixth Street, bartenders and waiters and busboys arrive as bar lights pop to life. They come sipping coffee, passing the architects and attorneys finishing their day's work. Happy hour and open doors and early family eaters at the rooftop Mexican restaurant.

Already music roars, shaking floors in still empty bars.

I circle past the bars looking for Lyle, then a block north past the church and Agape and the Salvation Army. Crowds hover around the edges of the Arch and Salvation Army hoping to score a bed or a slice of floor. It's a lottery. Some don't even hope, they unroll their bags and sleep against the outside wall. Some are waving cars into empty parking spaces, collecting tips and promising to keep an eye on their Volvos and Nissans.

I circle back to the bars on Sixth. A circle, a swirl. Soon the bars are brighter than the dying sky. Soon those who didn't win the bed lottery are building makeshift camps on the sidewalk or disappearing under the highway or down into scrub by the shallow city creeks. And I know their faces. People I eat with, people I sit with. But I don't sit and I don't stop and I find myself circling again, looking for Lyle.

The crowds grow, and they circle Sixth Street too. Walking east on south side sidewalk and west on the north side.

Barkers and vendors yell out. Bark bark — not at me, I have nothing to buy with and they know it. They bark at the girls and boys and solo sick men offering shots and music and live comedy and cheaper drinks and louder music and possibility.

"Lyle!"

Now the street is late night screams and laughter and I'm caught again in the swirl and I'm circling and spinning and screaming for Lyle.

I am catching faces and scanning crowds. I am spinning, and I need Lyle, who will stop me.

I step fast to each pedicab driver hoping it's him. Some shirtless, one pantless, men and women each with calves like stone and faces long suffering, calling jokes to each other as they pass.

"Lyle?"

They spin past me, some with Christmas lights and portable stereos, some with Rasputin beards and long distance cackles.

It is the same path, again and again. The same circle—only deeper, tighter each time, burrowing down, narrowing as I descend from the top of the tornado down to the point where wind hits stone.

Job called it God. Job cowered before the winds and heard poetry.

On to the street where the people swerve and bounce against one another. The police have blocked the road from car traffic to allow the drunk and will-be drunk to hop and lope and fall and laugh at the broken heel in the grate and the cut chin.

"Lyle?"

Vendors call out order numbers from the safe boxes, handing out food to the pay-drunks and the skirts-fucks who reach out and grab their food as they swirl by, like a child reaching from a merry-go-round—only faster. They manage to grasp beer and tequila and tacos and pizza. And the cover bands play and teenagers rub and everything that should be glory and laughter is sick and doggish. And it's growing more hellish as two am approaches and the cops on their shitting horses know this. They stare down at the swirl, waiting and knowing they'll have to step in and chances are their horses will drown and be stripped of flesh and cooked on small fires under the embankments and between grease dumpsters and perhaps the smell of cooking horse will rise and offend the senses of the condo owners above.

The bar that sold nothing that night stares out angry and lonely and a woman with her face painted like an angel stands on a crate perfectly still and waits for tips and the beggars beg matter-of-factly, saving their better stories for daylight. A man pushes himself by his heels backwards in a wheelchair—one of two wheelchairs the beggars use down here. One belongs to a man who needs it. It's operated by his fingers, his only moving parts, and I can't fathom how he gets here each night or who laces the plastic crown on his head or who scribbled his note asking for dimes or who told him to smile smile smile. And the other wheelchair belongs to everyone and the homeless take turns snagging it from each other and spending a night sitting and patrolling with an open hand and a piece of cardboard reading *Anything Helps*.

Anything helps.

Some are trying to sleep in the swirl, curled figures in doorways, pushed against steps, heads covered, hands clinging, even in sleep, to a plastic bag of belongings—an extra shirt, perhaps an ID, a pay-as-you-go cell phone. And those spinning and dancing are clinging even as they spin. Clinging to bodies and cash and highs. Clinging and trotting, all in the same waters, the same spinning waters, and we are all going down and it makes no difference the shape of the scrapwood you cling to.

A family of four, in yellow sweaters, stands on the corner singing hymns and handing out tracts and their madness is as drunk and sad as those passing.

This girl's skirt is ripped and she doesn't know.

This man hoots anger, locking eyes with anyone and hooting, daring them, wanting a fist like it's food.

They spin, and the street spins.

There are ghosts too—howling and screaming and bleeding spirit up and down the road—but no one can hear them over the cover band or the wailing plump Latino girl who spills her purse or the fire truck sirens a half-mile away.

"Lyle!"

The back of the pedicab catches my ribs and knocks me down.

"Fucking drunk," the girl passenger says. Even as she passes I can smell her perfume like a burning field of roses.

The music plays from every door and roof and mixes like grease smoke in the streets. People cough from the sound.

I circle again, further in. Faces, pale and pool ball-eyed, stare up from storm drains, watching up as we circle, not yet risking to grab us. Waiting.

I should wash this all with gasoline and lye. Clean my hands with burn.

It's two am and the bars who have loved them and protected them have pushed them to the doors with orders to fly, but some can no longer walk. A couple—maybe eighteen—can't stand from the curb and the taxi they called won't find them and they'll be there at three with heads exploding and the street cleaners will sweep their brains but leave their corpses for the bulk pick up on Tuesday. They're all still circling, brainsick and staggering. These were my students! These were my children! I go to one boy. "Be careful! Be careful! They'll grab you from the gutters." He pushes me and laughs. I go to a girl, her dress like sausage casing pulled over her body. "Be careful!" She yelps and clings to her tall friend. Both stumble on their heels and scamper away with tiny clown steps.

People line the curbs calling to full taxis and cursing each other and begging for a slice of pizza or a kebab and the noise still swirls in a circle—the same direction, how does it move in the same direction?

I'm circling the center now. Spiraling to a point of no motion. The whirlpool takes me in. I think I'm crying. Someone is crying.

Someone seizes me from behind, wrapping his arms around me. They've come up from below to take me. The thing throws its weight against me, pushing me into a piss alley. I fall, my face hitting the cement behind a dumpster filled with rot. The dumpster blocks the din, and things are hushed. I'm expecting the grey, large-eyed faces, but it's two men standing above me. One wears an aqua-blue shirt. NO MEANS NO. He kicks at my head, misses and hits my throat.

"Shit, James. You kicked him in the throat."

"The fucker's squirming," one says. Then to me. "Stop squirming."

I don't squirm. I don't call out. And I look up and see the stars in the sky. It's quiet here.

NO MEANS NO kicks me in the face and I feel the grit of back teeth broken and he kicks me again while the other rips at my empty pockets.

The whirlpool is closing in now, I can see that. All eyes eventually close, even the eyes of storms.

I LAY STILL LONG AFTER THEY HAVE GONE. I LAY WITH MY FACE AGAINST the cement and the taste of rain and street and blood in my mouth. I lay wondering if the grey hollow dwellers will come for me now. I have no strength to fight them off.

When the thought to stand comes, I ask myself where I can go. Where can I be? Even Whataburger has turned me away. But I do stand and I do walk. My brain bobs in my wet skull and each step makes it slosh against the side. I'm walking north.

Two hours later, I see Martin's house.

My legs are string and glue. My feet burning bruises. I walk up the drive, past the Cadillac, and knock until Laika opens the door wearing white underwear and a tank top, her face lined with sleep.

"Oliver, what are you doing here? Your face, my God." She takes my hand and leads me in, past the kitchen and living room and through Sam's door. I flinch.

"He's not here," she says, but I scan the room as she sits me on the bed. "He's doing his comedy. He'll be gone till very late."

"Where do you sleep?" I ask.

"Here," she says. "Sometimes the couch."

She holds six Advil in her palm and a cup of water, feeding me like a child. The room has one bedside lamp with a red shade. Red shadows dissolve into black. She dabs my face with a wet hand towel.

"There is gravel in your cuts," she says. "Don't move."

And with slow hands she plucks the rocks from my skin. She doesn't ask who did this. She doesn't ask anything. She cleans away the grime, changing towels once, pushing my hair back.

"The peroxide will sting. Don't shout. You'll wake Martin."

I feel my face frothing as she pours. I close my eyes and listen to the bubbles.

"Thank you," I say.

"Always getting into messes," she says. "My daughter would cut her knee every week. Sometimes every day. Always coming home crying."

"Maybe she can move here without your husband. Come live with you."

"Where?" she says. "Here? In this room? Take off your shirt. Let me help."

Her hands on my shoulders. She's close, kneeling on the bed beside me. She's touching my face, studying my wounds.

"Things do not change unless we change them, yes?" Her hand moves into my hair, pushing back, her fingers pressing my scalp. I smell her sour body. I feel her heat through her tank top.

"You are sad always, like a Russian," she says. "In Russia they say America likes fat, like Russia likes sad."

"I don't love my son."

She is still.

"Are you angry?" she asks. "Angry that he died?"

"Another son. He's alive."

"And you do not love him?"

"I see him and I feel sick. He doesn't know me." I breathe in, my lungs heavy as sandbags.

She leans back, looking at me with grey eyes. She peels the tank top over her head and I stare, her body pale, tiny freckles on her white skin shoulders. She scoots on her knees toward me and holds her body to mine, her chest to my face.

"I wish he was dead," she says. "He will be drunk tonight and he will want to rape me." She rests her chin on the top of my head. I feel the air she breathes in.

"Laika."

"I have not lived well," she says. She strokes my hair, holding me tight to her. "But I do not deserve to be raped. Do I?"

"Laika, no," I say, my voice weak.

"Will you stay with me? Maybe Sam won't come tonight and you can stay? Yes?"

"Laika."

There's a rattle at the front door. She pushes me back, animal fear in her eyes. Sam cackles in the next room.

"He will kill you," she whispers, pulling me off the bed.

"I'll go. I'll—"

"No, no. He will kill you." She pulls me by hand to the open closet, pushing me inside. "No breathing. No sounds."

"But I'll be trapped."

"Take this." She puts a slender kitchen knife in the palm of my hand. Where did it come from? "Don't let him do this to me."

"Laika."

She speaks quickly in a sharp whisper. "I will hold him and you will cut him. He will be very drunk. It will be easy. Cut him across his neck. Cut deep." She's closes the closet door.

"I can't . . ."

She stares at me through the slits of the closed closet door. Just eyes free from her face and body.

"You and I will be together," she whispers. "We will have money and only you will I fuck. Yes?"

She nods, backing away, and I think, maybe it's not too late. Maybe I can escape. I hear Sam stumble down the hall. She's in the bed, her eyes staring at the closet, and I don't know if she can see me through the slits. I should run. I should run from this house. But before I can move, Sam is falling into the room, expelling a high-pitched drunken laugh.

"I killed tonight, baby," he slurs. "Nothing missed. The emcee was like, 'You slayed them, Sam.'"

"Quiet, Sam," she says, pretending to wake. "Martin is sleeping."

"Dying, more like it."

He trips to the bed, landing on her and laughing. She pushes him back.

"No, Sam. I don't want to."

He laughs louder, grabbing her.

"No, Sam." She shoves his hands off her. "I was asleep."

He slaps her hard, his face losing its laugh for a moment, then breaking into a grin again. "Come on, baby." He slaps her again.

Laika stops moving. She lays her arms by her side, shaking slightly as if she were cold.

"That's more like it, baby." He kisses her neck and shoulders. She stares up as he moves his mouth over her. And I watch and I don't what to do. He sucks on her breasts and she doesn't move. Bile bubbles in my throat, acidic and hot. I squeeze the knife.

"Undress me," he says, sitting up and moving to the edge of the bed. He waits, facing the closet. He stares directly at the door, at me, but he doesn't see me. Laika moves to her knees behind him, her cheek red from the slap. She reaches around him, unbuttoning his shirt from the top down.

"You should have seen me on the stage. You should hear those people howl." He moves his head somberly, his face drunk and slack. "I'm really good."

"Yes," she says. "You are good."

As Laika slowly works through the buttons, Sam mumbles through his routine. "Who here likes pussy? I'm crazy about the pussy." His voice is low and monotone and his head bobs, his eyes lids heavy.

Laika looks over his shoulder to me. Right at me. In one move she pulls the shirt down from the collar and holds it behind his back. Sam's arms, still in the sleeves, are pinned, his tattooed chest pushing forward. She's holding him for me. All I need to do is step out and slash. All I need to do is that, and I will save her.

"What the fuck?" he says, craning his neck to look at Laika. For now he can't maneuver out. I clutch the knife, my other hand on the closet doorknob. I want to do this. I want to do something. But murder? I squeeze the knife.

Sam throws back an elbow that catches Laika on the chin. She falls back. He stands, turning to her, his back to me. I could do it now.

"What the fuck was that all about?" He swings and slaps her head. "Don't make me fucking hit you."

"Sam, I—"

"Shut up." He crawls on to the bed. She tries to sit up and he slaps her down again. He rolls her over onto her chest, pushing his pants down to his thighs. Her face, pressed against the mattress, looks at me, her eyes empty. And I do nothing, even as he falls on her, even as he shoves himself into her. I do nothing to stop this. I do nothing. And she finally closes her eyes. My hand still squeezing the knife.

I wake on the floor of the closet. My face feels bloated, ready to burst, and my tongue scrapes itself against my broken teeth sending chill pains into my skull. I peek through the slits of the door. She's alone in the bed. I inch out of hiding. She's face down, sleeping, her dirty blond hair spread out on the pillow like an open palm. Through the narrow long window that runs across the side of the room I see it's still night.

I creak the bedroom door open. The television buzzes in the living room, but nothing moves. With my shoes in hand, I creep down the hall and peek around the corner. No one is there. Only the TV with two crying faces arguing in a crowded ballroom.

I move to the front door and reach for the knob. But something stops me.

I turn around. Martin's door is cracked open and a thin line of light shines out. I step toward it, thinking I shouldn't, thinking I should go. But I'm moving to Martin's room and I'm hearing it. Strained breath, something falls. And I push the door fully open.

Martin's legs kicking free from sheets and Sam, his shirtless back to me, leaning over him, his whole weight pushing a dirty pillow against Martin's face. Thin arms reach and scratch at Sam. It's silent, but Martin's body is screaming.

And I see the side of Sam's face, his jaw tight, his breath held. This is what he looks like fucking. There's hate in me like morning light and I've grabbed the golf club without realizing it.

I swing hard. On impact Sam's face thuds, parts giving way. He tumbles to the floor and I hit him again. He tries to get up and I bring the club down hard against his head. He tries to stand again, but falls back. Blood, more black than red, runs down his face. And the world is small and I am strong.

Martin coughs and mews like a newborn. I turn to see him clutching at his sheets. He's wet the bed. Sam groans on the floor and tries to say something. But it's mush. I've broken his jaw.

I kick him in the gut and watch the air gasp out of his wet mouth. I kick his face and his nose crunches. The club feels perfect in my hands. Everything feels perfect.

"Sam," I say. "I'm going to kill you." My voice is calm, almost kind.

"Ollie, he . . . Ollie," Martin says.

"I'm going to kill you right now and no person on earth will care."

Sam moans, trying to stand, pushing himself against the arm of the recliner, his head spilling from his nose and mouth.

"Ollie, wait," Martin is catching his breath.

I raise the club high.

"Ollie, stop it, damn it." Martin croaks. "I asked him to do it."

I turn. Martin stares at me, his chest heaving.

"I paid him to do it. I paid him." He's crying and coughing.

I turn to Sam. He's kneeling and coughing. The golf club hangs loose in my hand.

"Mutha fucker," Sam says through his broken mouth. He's climbing up the recliner. "I'm gonna fucking kill you."

I think I should move. And I think I should do something. Then I think I should do nothing.

"Okay," I say.

He stands, blood dripping onto his chest, his rodent tattoo now a slaughtered pig.

He'll kill me now and that's all right.

Sam teeters for a moment. I drop the golf club.

"Mutha fucker," he says. I nod. He lunges forward and I see the surprise on his face before I hear the shit. It's a cracking white-hot noise.

Now the blood is red, bright as crayons. There's a hole just below Sam's neck, a little off center, the place where the collarbone presses against the skin. Sam stutter steps back, his mouth open in manic astonishment. He knocks into the stack of die-cast model cars and falls.

I watch him hit the floor before I turn to see her. She's frozen in the doorway, wearing only her white underwear, the gun still pointing at Sam's dead body.

SMOKY GOD

. . . A mammoth ball of dull red fire—not startlingly brilliant, but surrounded by a white, mild, luminous cloud, giving out uniform warmth, and held in its place in the center of this internal space by the immutable law of gravitation. This electrical cloud is known to the people "within" as the abode of "The Smoky God." They believe it to be the throne of "The Most High. —Olaf Jansen

Who is this that darkeneth counsel by words without knowledge

Then the Lord answered Job out of the Whirlwind

Who maketh the Clouds his Chariot & walketh on the Wings of the Wind

the Drops of the Dew

Hath the Rain

a Father &who hath begotten

WBlake invent & sculp

London. Published as the Act directs March 8.1825 by William Blake, N⁴ 3 Fountain Court Strand

Proof

MARTIN SITS IN THE LIVING ROOM, HIS MOUTH OPEN AND HIS EYES the yellow of tree sap.

Laika shivers on the couch across from him. I have turned off the television and given her a blanket, which she does not touch.

"I hate your country," she says. "I was poor in Russia. Here I am poor and a whore and a murderer."

"It's the land of opportunity," I say.

"Please don't talk. When you talk you say horrible things."

I look for tea or coffee in the kitchen but find only a few packets of sugar. I boil water on the stove and make three mugs of steaming water, adding half a packet of sugar into each.

Martin sips his and I sit beside him.

"He's dead?" he asks.

Sam's corpse is curled in the shower stall. I nod. Martin frowns.

"He wasn't so bad, you know?"

I do not respond.

Laika pulls her knees to her chest.

"Martin," I say. "If I call the police, someone is going to jail."

"Jail ain't so bad," he says.

"I'm guessing they'd deport her."

"Good. She wants to go home."

"And then they'll put her in jail."

"Russian jails are very bad," she says from behind her knees.

Martin stares forward, his scum eyes and his cheeks falling inward. I once read that those on the edge of life—newborns and the dying— reflect the shine of heaven. What a load of horseshit.

"I'm going to clean this up, Martin."

He nods.

"I'll need a car."

"Take the Caddy," he says.

"It drives?"

"Sam got it running. Got tires, too," he says, his voice weak. "He wasn't so bad." He looks up at me. "No tags or inspection, so you'll get a ticket if you get pulled over."

I glance toward the bathroom. "I'll be careful."

Martin pats my leg, looking at the smoke-stained carpet.

"I'm sorry," he says. "I did all this." He looks up at Laika. "I'm sorry to you, too." Then turns his face to me. "I'm just so done, Ollie. Just done."

I take his small face in my hands. I stare into his eyes and say as slowly and clearly as I can, "Martin, you are completely forgiven."

And he's nodding and crying, his head shaking between my palms.

EVERYTHING FEELS VERY REAL. VERY SHARP. IT'S MY FIRST TIME behind a wheel in close to three years and it feels right. My stomach bubbles with panic, but I'm moving and the movement pushes thinking to the back of my brain.

I knock on Lyle's door for fifteen minutes before he opens.

"Whoa, what the fuck happened to you?"

"Lyle, I said some cruel things in front of Horner," I say. "I'm sorry."

He nods, not acceptance, just an acknowledgment.

"Where you been?" he asks. "You look like shit?"

"I need your help," I say. "I tried to call—"

"My pedicab got clipped by a truck. Broke my phone. Broke my bike. I got road rash."

"Ouch."

"I look better than you," he says. He considers me for a beat. "Give me ten minutes and I'll meet you downstairs."

I'm waiting in the Cadillac when he comes down. The engine is running.

"So you drive now?" he says, climbing into the passenger seat.

"I really am sorry, Lyle."

"Can I smoke in your car?"

"Sure."

"Then all is forgiven."

He lights up as I steer us out of the parking lot.

"Monday's the last day to pay Horner," he says, exhaling a cloud of smoke. "Not that you care." He glances at me, trying to gauge my reaction. "Still think it's solid?"

"I think it's worse," I say. "Maybe it's best we're not going."

"Fuck that," Lyle sucks in and breathes out. "Even if it's pitch-forks and dragons, I want to see it."

"Lyle," I say. "You told me you once killed a man."

"Two. And I'm not proud. But it was me or them."

"And you hid the bodies?"

"Fuck yeah." He flips down the visor and examines the mirror. "It's all about keeping a calm head."

"I have a corpse in the trunk."

He flips the visor closed, but says nothing.

"I have a corpse in the trunk," I say again.

"A human corpse?"

I nod.

"Stop the car."

"Lyle, I can explain—"

"Pull over and stop the car."

I ease the car to the shoulder and stop.

"Open the trunk," he says.

I press the trunk release and he climbs from the car. I hear his muted "Fuck" from inside. He crawls back in.

"You got a guy with half a neck wrapped in a shower curtain! What the fuck?"

"What happened to calm heads? Just tell me what did you do last time?"

"Last time? What last time?"

"The two men you killed."

"Fuck, fuck, Ollie. That didn't happen. You fucking know that."

"What would you do?"

"Shit, I want no part of this. Nothing."

"Listen, a good woman killed a bad man. That's all. I need your help. You are the smartest man I know, Lyle."

"I'm a fucking idiot, Ollie. You're an idiot to think I'm not an idiot."

"Think. What would you do?"

He nods fast, thinking.

"Alligator farm!" he says.

"Alligator farm?"

"Sure! We dump him. He's alligator shit by morning."

"Where do we find an alligator farm?"

"I don't know, Google?"

Honk. Someone behind us flashes headlights. We both turn back. The trunk is still open.

"Shit, shit, shit," Lyle squeaks.

We both jump out of the car. The headlights drop to parking lights. "Hey, need some help?" A small bald man smiles as he rolls down the window of his Prius. "You know your trunk is open?"

"What's it to you, fucker!" Lyle screams. I slam the trunk closed.

"I was just trying—"

"Well just try *trying* to fuck off!"

He does. Passing by, his ghostly face blurred behind the streaks of rain, he shoots us the finger and I feel sorry for him.

"Lyle," I say, walking back to the car door. "Let's go for discreet."

"I *am* discreet!" he turns. "And I'm driving. You don't even have a fucking permit."

We climb back in and he taps his forehead like it's a radio on the fritz.

"You don't have to do this," I say.

"Right? Like you're going to do it on your own."

"I got this far."

"Let me think, Ollie! Let me think."

He sits with hands on the unmoving wheel. "I'm going to be sick." He jumps from the car, vomits on the shoulder, and returns.

"Okay, okay," he says. "We read the obits, right. We find out when a funeral is happening, then we head to the cemetery after the burial. We dig up the fresh grave and place this guy on top of the coffin. See? See? They'll never find him."

I shake my head.

"Fine. Fine," Lyle stares at me. "Let's think. Something simple. Something elegant."

"Burn him," I say.

He faces the windshield, nods, and starts the car.

The HEB grocery store is too bright and the muzak too loud for six AM. Lyle and I walk in from the rain passing the cashiers and the few morning shoppers.

"Going to be a great cookout, huh?" he says loudly, clearly. He nudges me.

"Sure," I say. "The best."

"You get the chips. I'll get the dogs."

"Really?" I whisper.

"Meet you back here with the goodies!" he says, his eyes screaming for me to act my part.

I head down the aisles and grab a bag of potato chips. Then head back to the front but Lyle spins around the corner onto my aisle with a cart half filled with plastic wrapped hotdogs.

"How many have you got?" I ask.

"Enough."

"Enough for what?"

"To feed all the people . . . at our cookout . . ." Again, the screaming eyes. "What have you got?"

I look in my hand. The one bag I've grabbed is a single serving of Lays, the kind you find in brown-bag lunches. He shakes his head and glances around. The stocker, an old man with a goiter, has just moved into our aisle.

"Oh!" Lyle says loudly, cheerfully. "We'll need lighter fluid." He winks at me. "Let's grab a few extra bottles to be on the safe side."

We roll up to the cashier with forty-eight hotdogs, nine bottles of lighter fluid and one single serving of Lays potato chips. We smile as the cashier rings us up.

"Fifty-two dollars."

Lyle looks at me. I shake my head. He opens his own wallet. A twenty.

"Shit," he mutters. He pulls all the hotdogs out of the stack.

"Thirty two."

He takes two lighter fluid bottles out.

We leave with seven lighter fluid bottles and one bag of chips.

"Restock!" the cashier calls out as we leave.

Lyle rips open the chips.

"Lays? I hate these," he says, cramming a handful in his mouth. "No personality. Doritos have personality."

"It's raining."

"Perfect. No would suspect we'd burn a body in the rain. It makes no sense. The question is where. Where is no one surprised to see a fire?"

"Campgrounds?"

"Yes!" he snaps. "Know any?"

We drive an hour and a half into the hill country west of Austin toward Inks Lake. The land rolls as the morning fades in and the rain tempers. Lyle drives, chain smoking and gripping the wheel.

We pulled in to Inks Lake State Park a few minutes past seven—the day glowing gray.

Carrie and I camped here once. An early date—marshmallows, box wine in plastic cups, awkward lovemaking in a tent.

A young ranger greets us at the entry.

"Morning! You're the first folks of the day."

"We'd like a nice secluded spot," Lyle says.

"Great. Plenty open. The rain usually keeps folks away." She points out Spot 47 on a crude map and asks us for thirteen dollars.

"Thirteen?"

"Yep."

We pause. Then it hits me.

"Pop the trunk," I tell Lyle. His face dies. "Just pop it."

I climb from the car and make my way to the back, smiling at the ranger. There's Sam's body in the shower curtain, the blood congealed like overnight egg yolk. I reach around his body to his back pockets and find a wallet. I open it and sure enough there's a stack of bills. I pocket the bills, close the trunk, and hand a twenty to the ranger.

"Left my money in the trunk," I say.

The ranger smiles and nods. "Sure. Safest part of the car."

Spot 47 sits behind some pines, with a brief walk down to the lake. The neighboring sites are empty for now. We are unseen.

Our map tells us to keep all fires in designated fire pits. It's not a large pit—a four-foot circle of gray bricks. We lift Sam from the trunk and squeeze him into the pit, wrapping his body around itself in a fetal position. Sam's mouth is open, as if he's yawning. We cover him with branches and moss, then douse the whole pile with three bottles of lighter fluid.

Lyle flicks his lit cigarette on top.

Nothing happens.

"I thought it would . . . boom," he says.

He reaches in with his lighter, lighting the corners of leaves. The lighter fluid catches and the leaves crackle, but the branches and the body merely smolder, giving out a wet, gray smoke.

"Come on! Burn!" Lyle says, circling the pit. "At this rate we're just making jerky."

"Give it time."

"In *Conan the Barbarian* it just explodes, you know? Just BOOM! Fire!"

I sit and watch the pile. The body can't be seen under the brush, the trash, the debris. Just one finger, sticking out like a twig.

Lyle sprays on another bottle of lighter fluid. A few flames lick to life, but hardly last.

I sit, Lyle paces. After an hour and he's nearly frantic.

"Look," he says. "We need more lighter fluid. Something. Give me the cash and I'll make a run. You watch him."

I reach into my pocket, but pause. I look at Lyle bouncing on the balls of his feet.

"You'll come back, right?"

"Jesus, Ollie. Just give me the money."

I hand him the money and he climbs into the Cadillac.

AN HOUR PASSES. AND ANOTHER. STILL THE PIT IS LITTLE MORE THAN smoke and Lyle is nowhere.

I pour another bottle of lighter fluid on before I realize I don't have a lighter.

I sit on the ground and think. Could I drag him to the lake? Could I feed him to wolves?

I think about Martin and Laika, about her touching my face, about Martin's face in my hands.

Martin wanted to die. It's a strong sick that overcomes that simple desire to live. Even when the time came and Sam pressed down the pillow, Martin fought. Some basic brain took over and scratched and clung. That's not how he wanted to go, suffocated in his bed. No one wants to die like that.

Sam wanted to live. He wanted to perform stand up and watch documentaries and whore out immigrants and beat on dying men. Now he's dead. I feel something different from guilt. I feel responsible. It's not a horrible feeling.

Three hours have passed. It begins to drizzle and even the smoke is dying away.

I walk down to the lake watching the slow rain dimple the surface. The surface beginning still, but rippling constantly. The universe must look like this to some eternal eyes—each dimple a star appearing, expanding, and then gone. I look down and see my feet are in the water.

I had thought this moment would be one of passion and panic—a squeezed trigger, a fast step, all before I could change my mind. I had thought I would have to move quickly enough to outrun the part of me that opposed the act. The part of me that wanted life. But here I am and there is no conflict. No part of me to outrun.

I slip from my sandals and step deeper. My pant legs soak up the cold.

It doesn't feel like a choice. It feels wonderfully inevitable. Perhaps I've stepped back onto God's path. The thought makes me smirk.

I take another step. Step. Still so beautiful. Leaves float down like whispers. Step.

The water is cold to my crotch, like the neighbor's pool when I was ten years old. Friends calling "Don't walk in, jump."

Step. Sludge squeezing into my shoes.

Owl hoots. Church camp. Age nine. Walking alone to pee in the middle of the night—night like I'd never known night. Hoot.

Step. Mud sucks against my feet, holding me back, but only half-heartedly. I pull free and step on.

This is not disdain for life. This is only knowing it's over.

Water just below my ribs. I'm sending ripples just like the stars.

She and I walked on a golf course at night, silent as beech bark, nervous as sparrows.

This is not sad. Nor is this peace. This is simply how things are.

My chin dips in. Sounds bounce off the surface from all around me. Raindrops and bird calls and insect hums and wind through weeds and snippets of pop songs and my father calling for me to refill his coffee, my mother cooing as she sees me wearing my best suit, my dormmate's girlfriend climaxing in the dark four feet away, my puppy whining in his bath, Carrie sighing on a cold October day, Miles laughing at a puppet made of socks and rubber bands and I laugh and water spills into my mouth and I cough and spit and I step forward.

The world goes from blue gray to moss green. Ear bubbles and muffled all. Let my feet sink deeper. Let the mud hold me under. The universe is not killing me. The universe is not saving me. The universe is just here, awesome and transient.

Open my mouth. Let the green into the lungs.

A yapping false panic like a child begging not to go to bed even though the sun is down and day is done.

Acid in my throat. Panic.

Pine needles floating on an ice blue pool and hotel towels stacked liked sugar cubes. The water tastes like pennies in my mouth.

Panic keeps screaming, a hysterical old woman in my chest.

I'm eighteen and the rope swings from deck into the river—but you must let go! You must or you slam back into the deck cutting both knees. And she's below me and she's bored and I should finish soon. And Carrie and I so drunk we sweat gin and bacon and the sheets smell of everything.

Blink. Miles, little man. My Miles. Miles waiting. Waking alone. Miles calling out. Calling for me. Afraid and calling for me. You're calling for me. I do not come. You're calling for me and I do not come. I do not come and I do not come and forever I do not come.

If I love more. If I love more.

This lake is every face of every corpse. This water is thick with us.

I'm yanked out of the green and wet into a world brighter and louder.

I thrash against the hold, pushing and kicking. But whatever has me will not relinquish its hold. It pulls me back, arms around my chest, above the water.

He pulls me out of the water as I cough and heave.

"What the fuck are you doing?" Lyle throws me down on the bank. "We're working here. We're working."

He grabs his hair and paces in front of me.

"God damn, God damn. I'm gone for ten minutes and you're ready to off yourself."

I sit up, coughing up lake water spiked with stomach acid. "You've been gone more than three hours."

"So you decide to kill yourself?"

"It wasn't about you."

"Well it is now, fucker, I just saved you."

"What about it being time to leave the party? What about walking out with my head high?"

He looks suddenly serious. "You have cancer?"

"No, Lyle, you idiot."

"So your son died. I'm sorry! Big fucking deal . . . . I mean it is a big fucking deal. But it's not the only deal. It's not the only thing. Move on, you fuck."

I shake my head.

He stomps to me and picks me up off the ground.

"What are you doing?" I ask.

He steps into the water and lugs me into the lake.

"Go ahead and drown, dead man."

He turns back, marching back toward the campsite. I stand and run at him. I'm yelling as I slam into his back, knocking him to the ground. I pound fists into his back, into his kidneys.

"You piece of shit, Lyle, you stupid piece of shit."

Lyle bucks under me, but I hold on. He twists, but I jab fists into his ribs. He reaches a hand behind him and grabs a handful of my hair and pulls me off. Then he's on me, slapping my face. We tumble back into the lake. I trip back and he has me pinned. He holds me down, water lapping over my face. He shoves me down, holding me under, back of my head sinking into the mud, and his face blurry above, blurry above. And I can't breathe and I have nothing. His hands are heavy on my chest, holding me under.

He yanks me up. "Do you want to die?"

I suck at the air, but I'm down again and sucking water instead.

He pulls me up again.

"Do you want this? Oliver? We can do it right now!"

Down again. And my lungs are lurching, pushing out and sucking in water.

He yanks me out again.

"Live or die, fucker. Last chance, Oliver. Last chance."

My voice blotched and high. "Live."

Lyle holds me by my shirt staring down at me, he's breathing hard, his teeth stained yellow, his eyes narrow and frightened. He pulls me to a sitting position. And we're both sitting waist deep in the muddy waters.

"Good," he says. "Good."

"I GOT START 'EM STICKS, BURN-O-LOGS, LIGHTER FLUID." HE throws open the back door of the Cadillac. "I got us some food and beer, too." He tosses me a can of Pringles.

"Did you think about not coming back?"

"No," he says, facing me. He's lying, I can see that. But he's also here.

"Thank you," I say, holding up the Pringles.

"I saved the best for last," he says and pulls two five-gallon tanks of gasoline from the back seat. "Let's get this fire started."

He opens up one of the tanks and circles the pit pouring. He lights a cigarette, takes a few puffs, and flicks it onto the pile.

Whoomp. Fire swells up eight feet high.

"See? Now that's some barbarian shit."

You can see him through the burning. His clothes burn first. Then his hair and skin. I can just see one opossum claw curl, like the animal is gripping at the flames. Soon he's not Sam anymore.

The fire burns away the branches and trash, exposing more of his shrinking body, the flesh pulling back from the teeth and eye sockets, the skin wincing tight.

"Jesus, God," Lyle says, breaking branches from trees and throwing them on top. "Jesus, don't look at that."

But I do look. I won't not look. Because I put him there in that pit and I'm burning him, so I'll watch.

The rain comes and goes and Lyle eats Doritos and Marshmallow Peeps and sucks down beer.

Things pop and bubble in the fire. The smoke is oily, greasy to the skin.

A family of campers hike by, calling from the road, "Smells delicious!"

And it does. A barbecue sweet smell that makes my mouth water in spite of me.

I shift the coals and the logs, keeping the heat high, throwing in the Start Em Sticks and lighter fluid, keeping the orange and red moving over the charred body.

The sun sinks and Lyle is out of cigarettes and panicking.

"Go buy some," I suggest.

"I spent all the money."

"Well, it's a good night to quit."

"Fuck you."

It's a gray dusk that moves quickly into black, heralded by hoots and chirps. And the bugs swarm, mad for the smell, nipping and drinking and Lyle slaps himself over and over, leaving his neck red.

We sit silent as he drinks beer and I watch the fire. He grows bored and sick and crawls into the back seat of the Cadillac with the last beer.

And I'm alone with Sam's body. So much less than Sam now. Less than Sam's corpse, even. Just a loose combination of meat that once moved and talked. Black bones and burning gristle and parts I don't recognize. I don't move from the flames. I sit and watch the yellow and red and orange and the leather squeezing dry around the bones.

It's dark outside the circle of firelight and bugs chant a rhythmic hum.

I know his questions are done. His thinking is done. His *all* is over. And I add more fuel and I think perhaps if it was me lying there my dying would cost the world nothing. My absence would mean nothing at all. I suppose that was always true, but the world and I conspired to keep it a secret from me for most of my life. Maybe a handful would miss me. But they'd die too before long.

I was first to find Miles.

Christmas morning in his cot, his body still, empty. I touched him and smelled him and I knew. But I also didn't know. I grabbed him to me, a cool, plastic non-ness. Something invisible, something internal in the world ripped. They wouldn't let me keep him, that was what my brain screamed, they won't let me keep him. They don't let you keep the body.

Miles alone. The dark of his room. The quiet roar of white noise. Did he call out for me? Did he call out for his dad?

That means something. It is in my throat. I know not one thing in this world as holy as Miles's heart seizing up and his breath failing.

That is holy.

More than meaning, Miles. Beyond meaning. Holy.

And this man burning is holy.

I promise you, Miles, you and me and Sam and my guilt and all anyone in anyplace ever loved ever ever ever all transient as smoke and holy as daybreak.

The heat and smoke swirl and my eyes blur. The rain slows to a stop. I look up at the branches stretched across the moving sky, twisting and curling like dark water cutting a dozen streams into the sandy clouds. Exhaustion circles me like a viper, darting in with sudden snaps of sleep. I keep my eyes on the fire, but the flames change, the body shifts. Under the cracking and clucking of the burn is a voice-like hissing. A secret whispered.

You cannot send me. You must take me.

"Where," I reply.

And he sits up, his face veined in red and orange, his grin lipless and white. He leans forward until the smell of his hot dead flesh fills my nose.

Wake up.

And I do. He's not sitting. He's not talking. He's only a body curled beneath burning logs. It's clear now, this body is not going to burn away. The fire is too small, the body too thick, the air too wet.

Lyle doesn't stir as I remove the shower curtain from the trunk. It takes some time removing Sam from the fire. I use a corner of the curtain as an oven mitt and pull at his shoe, a gooey melted mess. I snatch and tug, like removing a baked potato from the oven. Bit by bit, I drag the body—most of it—from the fire pit and onto the curtain. I wrap it around him, cinching the curtain with my belt. I take hold of one end and walk, dragging Sam behind me, from the light of the fire and into the dark of the night.

The shower curtain crackles as it scrapes against the gravel road, sounding hideously loud in the quiet. When I pause to catch my breath, the plastic settles, like insects scurrying over paper.

I turn from the road and push into the cedars and brush. Branches snag at my hair and scratch against my cheeks, but I keep moving, away from the road, climbing up at a slight incline. The ground is stony and hard, the cedar roots protruding in and out like frozen sea serpents, as if the ground were constantly rejecting the roots and the roots were just as vigilantly pushing back in.

I walk into a clearing where the ground has won and I drag Sam on, making white noise against the rootless soil. From here I can make out the expanse of inky underbrush surrounding me. Far to the east I can see the white promise of the rising moon. Down the opposite side of the hill I've climbed, I see a small cliff and in the side of the cliff, a cave, small and black.

I make my way down, Sam dragging behind me. It's not so much a cave as a crack, as wide as the width of a man. I have to duck to enter and maneuver Sam's body so he can squeeze through. Inside smells of cool, wet stones, a fresh loamy scent. As dark as it was outside, it's darker still. I move deeper in.

The hole widens the further I move in. I glance back and the opening crevice is now a strip of lighter shade. I move forward, my eyes adjusting somewhat, but the dark is so rich, so nearly complete that I am close to walking blind. I could just drop the body here, but I don't, I drag it deeper in. Soon, even the light of the entrance is gone.

In the dark, I can feel the ground steadily decline. Occasionally the curtain slips from my sweating hands and I have to grope in the dark until I find it again.

My breaths echo back to me, the sound made strange. But I'm not afraid. I'm keenly awake. The ground is steeper now, rockier. The curtain snags on a stone and I imagine creatures nipping at the ends, pulling it back, cave-dwelling rodents, blind and hungry, crawling from the cracks and scratching at the body. Or maybe I hear them chattering, whispering. I do not stop. My movement keeps them at bay.

My throat is dry and my skin tingles, but I keep moving on. I could be a mile in, more. I can't tell. I walk on, letting the decline pull my legs. Then the ground evens out and my steps catch the rhythm of my breathing. And now I do hear something, or more accurately, feel something. A vibration, a hum. I come to what seems like an end—a wet, rock wall. But I don't turn back. I grope along the wall searching for a way to go deeper. Low to the ground, I find a horizontal gap. I push Sam in first, then press my body to the ground to squeeze after him.

It's awkward and slow, pushing the body ahead of me inch by inch. The space narrows. Sam won't move. I can't move. I cannot move. And the chattering from somewhere. I maneuver around Sam's body, crawling beside him. And then we are face to face, buried beneath a mile of stone, his face pressed against the thin plastic. And for the moment I'm not afraid. I'm just here. And the chattering is nothing but crickets and wind.

I stare at Sam for several minutes before I realize I can seem him. There's light—subtle, but undeniable. I look ahead. The light seems to be coming from a shelf of glow only feet beyond me. I crawl on, reaching back and pulling Sam free.

I turn my head, squeezing and scrapping against the rock beneath me, pulling myself on and then I pull myself out, to my knees, to my feet. I breathe in, then kneel, reach back into the crevice and yank Sam out.

My eyes slowly adjust, and I see a large cavern glowing. I look up expecting some hole letting the moonlight in, but there's nothing but the high cavern ceiling. I walk on, my eyes growing more accustomed to the low light. And now I see the source. In the center of the cavern is a pool, green-blue and utterly still. It glows.

I leave Sam's body and step to the edge and look down. I startle at the face, but it's only mine. The surface is still as glass and reflects my face like a mirror. My eyes surprise me, my pupils wider and dark as if my insides might spill out. I watch my face, scraped and bleeding, then let my eyes focus past my reflection, and beyond me I see the emptiness of the water illuminated by something deeper. A few specks float, catching the soft light. All of me seems to slow as if I'm floating, too. And deeper still, miles and miles deeper, I see light. A gold and fiery sourceless light, a nothing glow.

There it is, the hum, the joy, the center. All the names and all the nameless.

I tip Sam's body over the edge and watch him sink away, past the still, past the miles, into the glowing and gone. I could sink down, too. Submerge in this pool and drop deep enough that I reemerge below. But I won't. I am still of this world, a world of touch and being. I understand that now.

I lower my face into the water. Questions—all my questions—don't apply. It would be like asking music to hold my hand. And though there's no face to see and I have no words to say, I am praying. I'm praying in all directions. What I'm given is enough. Seeing this enough. This—what is it? Love? It's too weak a word, but there is no other. This love. This radiant hollowness.

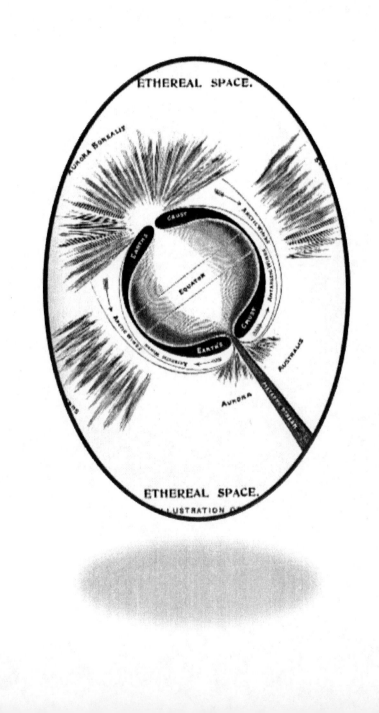

RETURN

It is now one hour past midnight—the new year of 1908 is here, and this is the third day thereof . . . I shall not live to see the rising of another sun. —Olaf Jansen

I LET LYLE SLEEP AS I STOMP THE FIRE OUT AND SHOVEL THE ASH INTO a trash bag. The moon is sinking when I finally load the last of our camp and head out. Lyle whimpers and snores in the back. I've given him new nightmares.

The drive is quiet, dark, the headlights hinting at direction. Austin glows white and yellow in the last of the night. I turn south toward pastel suburbs, and park along the curb outside a closed public pool, quietly climb from the car and leave Lyle sleeping.

In three blocks I reach her house. Their house.

I leave my shoes by the hedge and walk barefoot across the Augustine grass, letting blades skirt between my toes. I wonder if they have a dog. Carrie always wanted a dog.

The back door is guarded by a menagerie of small plants and muddy children's shoes. My first guess is the drooping cactus in the HOWDY pot. I lift it and find a single silver key. Finding it feels like touching a woman in a way you know will make her sigh, because you know her and she has shown herself to you. I turn the key and step into the house. This is watching your lover when she is alone. The kitchen smell of toast and flowers, the notes and child art on the fridge.

Half-played board games, unread mail, and an aquarium bubbling blue and green fill the living room. No furniture from our home made it here, but other bits and pieces did—the wooden cutting board in the kitchen, a few books on the shelves. With the mis-logic of a dream, elements of our life position themselves in new places, new contexts, new meanings. To the side of the mantle is our elephant—the white heavy piece Jeffrey clung to years before. I pick it up. Heavy—heavier than I remember.

Up the stairs, carpet soft as grass. The air hums quiet. One soft hall light. Three doors, all ajar. At the end of the hall I push the door open. It's darker inside. Her breaths I recognize. His breaths are just short of snores. On his nightstand lies a hardback topped with his round-rimmed eyeglasses and his wallet.

I open the wallet, and find, as promised, a cashiers check for five thousand and fifty dollars. I place it in my pocket and move to her side. She still sleeps on the left side. She still sleeps belly down. Her t-shirt rolls halfway up her back. She slept in the nude before. All before. I watch her sleep. I watch them sleep.

I kneel down beside her, her face inches from mine, her mouth barely open. I lean in close to smell her breath—sweet, white bread smell.

"I am sorry." I noiselessly mouth the words. "I am so sorry."

Her mouth closes, her dry lips clinging to one another.

I close my eyes. I want to sleep, to leave my head here and sleep inches from her face like I've done a thousand nights. I know now that in the end we give our souls to those we hurt as much as to those we love.

"Daddy?"

He stands in the doorway, the silhouetting hall light making him a solid shadow.

"Daddy?"

I open my mouth to answer. But it's not my voice I hear.

"Okay, Archer, okay," Manuel mumbles as he climbs from the

other side of the bed. He walks to the boy. The boy places a hand into his.

"I need to pee," he says.

The two walk down the hall and turn into the bathroom at the top of the stairs. I creep after them and stand outside the door listening.

As the water refills the tank—a long sustained hush ending in a bubbled burp—I back down the stairs. I stay in the shadows and watch Manuel carrying Archer, sleepy eyes and mussed hair. Manuel holds him to his chest, a hand beneath him and another across his narrow back. When they walk down the hall I step into the light just enough to see. The boy is already asleep on his father's shoulder.

After three years of living in the hollow earth, Olaf and his father prepared for home. They were gifted gold and a ship of supplies. They had entered in the north. But you can't leave the same way. The current drove them down, as deep into the center as one can go, and they emerged in the south.

They laughed aloud at the blue in the sky, remarking that for all the wonders within the hollow earth, that particular color was not to be found. The world—our world—looked surreal to the two men.

Relearning the stars, they charted a course for home. But an iceberg, warmed by the south summer sun, calved before them and shattered the boat. Olaf watched his father, caught in a web of rope, sink with the ship and gold. Olaf remained stranded on the iceberg itself—a lifeless, salt-ice island.

He would have died within a day and his story with him, but a passing whaling ship took him on, amazed to find a solitary man alive on the ice, asking how he came to be there.

He shared his story: the journey north with his father, the mazes of blue and white ice, the thrashing lip and swirling whirlpool, the race of wise singing beauties, and the red inner sun they worshipped as a god. He described the gold, the teachings, and the return to the surface.

What did he look like to those whalers? Had his skin a strange tint from his years under the misty inner sun? Had the fruit of that land and the inner air changed his face, his eyes? Something was different. They saw the change. Olaf was thrown into a madhouse for twenty-seven years.

I PULL UP IN FRONT OF LYLE'S APARTMENT BUT KEEP THE MOTOR RUN-ning.

"You don't want to come in and clean up?" he asks.

I shake my head. "I think you've had enough of me for one day."

"Maybe we keep low for a while. See how things pan out."

"That's a good idea," I say.

He opens the car door, his body moving slow, and I wonder if he regrets ever first approaching me in that bookstore.

"Thank you," I say.

He nods his head. "Just another day in the life." He climbs out, closing the door.

"Hey Lyle," I say through the window and he turns back. "If you do ever find a way in, send me a postcard, okay?"

"Yeah, well," he says, shrugging a little. "I'll keep trying."

He turns and walks toward the building. At his door, he'll search for his key and find a folded piece of paper. It will be a cashier's check for five thousand and fifty dollars. I hope he goes north. I hope he talks Jim Horner's ear off. I hope he discovers everything.

IT'S NOT YET DAWN WHEN I walk up the drive to MARTIN'S HOUSE. The front door swaying in the night wind and the drawn curtains over open windows catching gusts and billowing in to the living room.

Inside Laika sits on the couch, still in her underwear and tanktop, her gray eyes are like snow and sun. A green and white shoebox lies on her lap.

"Laika."

She looks at me, confused, but only for a moment. "You look even worse," she says. Her voice rings odd.

"I need a shower."

In the bathroom, I undress. My clothes are ripe with smoke and lake. The shower runs hot and I step in, letting the water scald my back, my scalp, my chest, letting steam fill my face and lungs. I stand until the water runs clear beneath me and my skin is free of the oil and blood.

"I found you some clothes," Laika says from the other side of the shower curtain. Again, her voice sounds strange.

When I climb out, she isn't there. But a neat pile of Martin's clothes are. Older clothes—a pair of worn jeans, a thin black sweater. They would hang loose on him. On me they fit snug but comfortable.

"Have you eaten?" I ask, stepping back into the living room. She's back on the couch, the blanket wrapped around her, staring into the space before her as if she's reading the air. "Laika, have you eaten since I left?"

"My name's not Laika."

Her accent is gone—that's what rings strange.

"I'm not Russian. I'm from Fort Worth."

I place a hand on the counter.

"I needed a better story. Something exotic. Who wants a Fort

Worth hooker?" She looks to me. "Would you have helped me kill him if I wasn't some exotic damsel in distress?"

"I didn't kill him."

"You hid the body. That's the part I couldn't figure out." She opens the shoebox and lifts out a stack of bills. "Eight hundred dollars, more or less. I thought there'd be more. Want to split it?"

"Your daughter."

Her lips twist, a frown that nearly smiles. No daughter.

"Laika was the cosmonaut dog. First dog in space," she says. "You really should have known."

"Martin? Does he know?"

"Martin's gone."

I turn down the hall toward Martin's room.

"He's not here," she calls out.

The bed is bare. The rug is gone.

"He couldn't breathe. He was turning blue." She walks into the room with me, staring at the bare bed. "I cleaned everything before anyone came. Cleaned it all up."

"Where is he, Laika?"

"I told you, that's not my name."

"Is he dead?"

"The ambulance came hours ago. He was alive then."

I push past her and out.

"I didn't lie about him stealing from Martin and beating me," she says as I reach the door. "I'm happy he's dead. I've never been so happy."

A FEW STARS STILL FLAKE THE WESTERN SKY. THE EAST JUST HINTS pale. The hospital hums electric.

I have no idea which room I'll find him in. It's long before visiting hours, I know.

I maneuver past the not-yet opened gift shop and the just-waking cafeteria, past halls of plastic plants and pastel landscapes and I find the one-room multi-faith chapel. I steal a bible.

The nurse behind the information counter looks tired. She scribbles too hard into her metal clipboard. I pull down the sleeves of my black sweater and smile.

"Morning, sister," I say.

She looks up at me with the weary eyes of a toll collector.

"I'm looking for Martin Dale."

"Are you immediate family?" she says.

"Spiritual family." I raise the bible. "I'm his pastor."

She nods, bored, then gives me a room number.

He lays beneath a white sheet in a cotton slip looking like a stain housecleaning missed. No window, no dawn sky, just florescent clean. I move to his side. Tubes in his nose. Tubes in his arms. Even a tube in his penis. Martin would hate this. As if he needs all this to die. He's dying just fine all on his own.

I place a hand on his chest.

I know this. I know this yellowing gray. His body is closing down, moving through the floors and switching off the lights.

I am his pastor, after all. A poor, broken clergy with a congregation of one and not a single sermon worth delivering. But I am his pastor. I will take on the responsibility of his Last Rites.

I remove the tube from the nose first, slowly sliding it out. Then the needle in his arm. Last the catheter, like removing a vein. Martin sleeps through it all.

I find an unattended wheelchair in the hall.

I slide my arms under Martin and lift him. He's light, like an armful of hanging suits, I lower him down into the chair and we roll from that room. I roll him past nurses stations and empty rooms and more plastic plants, onto an elevator with a grim-faced doctor who avoids looking at either of us, past the now-open gift store and the front desk and out into the new dawn sky.

No one even asks my name.

THE SKY MOVES FROM ORANGE INTO BLUE AS WE SPEED THROUGH THE hills. The windows are down and the air, clean from the rain, pours in pure.

The Cadillac has an old tape deck. I root around in the glove box and find an old Willie Nelson tape. Willie is singing about Poncho and Lefty, about federales and betrayal, about dying in Mexico.

Martin wakes once. His turns his head without lifting it.

"Ollie," he says, his voice dry as sand.

"Good morning, Martin."

"Doesn't she run pretty?"

"Like a dream, Martin."

He smiles at me, his eyelids heavy. "Where we going?"

"West," I say.

"Good, good." He watches the road as we crest another hill. Then looks back to me. "I'm dying," he says. It's half a statement, half a question.

"Yes," I say.

He nods and rolls his head back to the open window. The scent of cedar and oak fill the car. He closes his eyes.

"West is always beautiful," he says.

It is beautiful. The sky warming to blue, the road dry and clear, Martin with the wind in his face this one last time. I'll drive until his breathing stops. Then I'll drive some more. I'll drive until the road meets the ocean and the world reflects the sky.